FEDE  N

A Novel By

Allysha Hamber

Federal Prison Camp®

Federal Prison Camp

Is a work of fiction. Any resemblances to real people, living or dead, actual events, establishments, organizations, or locales are intended to give the fiction a sense of reality and authenticity. Other names, characters, places and incidents are either products of the author's imagination or are used fictiously. Those fictionalized events & incidents that involve real persons did not occur and/or may be set in the future.

Written by: Allysha Hamber
Edited by: Wendy Robinson
For information contact:
Allysha Hamber
Email: Allyshahahmber@hotmail.com
Website: www.allyshahamber.webs.com
Facebook.com/authorallyshahamber

Acknowledgements:

All my praises and honors are due to My Lord and Savior, who has brought me from such a mighty long way. Writing this book brought back a lot of memories and yes, a few were not so great but the majority were beautiful! Some of the women I met along this journey have touched my life in a way that even "family" could never do. We have shared the good, the bad and the ugly. We have comforted, cried, smiled, laughed, fought, made up, encouraged, uplifted, learned from and taught; simply loved one another on a level that most who have never experienced the confinement of prison could never understand.

I love each and every one of you for who you WERE to me and for those that still remain apart of my life, who you ARE to me and who you forever will BE to me. You helped me through some of my darkest hours and for that, I will be eternally grateful. God has smiled upon us to remain friends, keep in touch, watch one another's family grow and be able to say "I miss you" to someone who was such an instrumental part of one's life.

To my sister's: Shirley Delaney (Hey Sissy, love u!), Shannon Yost (Heyyy Bunkie!!! Love you!), Shanna Purnell, Valarie Merriweather (Hey lil' momma!), Simone Lowe, Robin Harris, Maggie Turpin (Hey Mommy, miss you!), Deborah Robinson, Sandra Mattox (Miss you so much! Love you to the moon and back!), Karmeletha Hatcher (Hey KK!), Keysha Murphy (Still killing the game on the outside!), April Cline (Words can't express what you mean to me wifey!), Roberta Deets (Always so sweet to everybody.. love that in you!), Ella Royal (Love you always!) Carla King (My crazy wild sister, miss u!) Tiny Mack (Thank you for putting so many smiles on our faces, Miss your sense of humor!), Wally Davis (Man, can you come take care of my hair??? Miss you), Edna Gooch (May God continue to shine through you!), My beautiful Baby Momma Shannon Rucker... Love you for all you've been to me, you are da bomb! Keep killing the game Boo!

To any of the ladies I missed, charge it to my head and not my heart! I'm so proud of each and every one of you! You took the lessons and experiences and applied them to this thing called life... and you shitting on the game and I LOVE IT!! Keep striving, never stop... but take a moment to look back every now and then, never forget the experiences we had... they had been instrumental in making us the strong, beautiful, positive and gifted women we are today... stay great!! I truly love you all!!!

Shouts out to: Author Mary L. Wilson (You are the most supportive woman I know! Love you Libra, keep doing what you do, you're awesome!), Shirlean Macklin (My sister from another mother, I love you dearly for all the love and support over the years!), Rhonda McAlister (Your belief in me has been so instrumental in developing who I am, Love you!), A.J Hogue (Blueeeeeee... many can never understand the love I have for you, for your belief in me and your support and love... Bluer than the ocean blue, I love you!,) Antoine DaOutsida (from the moment I met you in the club... lol.. you have been by my side, believing in me, pushing me and promoting me... you are so loved by me and I appreciate you to the moon and back!),

To that special person in my life: Life is never easy but when you have someone that makes your heart smile just at the sound of their voice, it helps to bring the best out of every day. I love you and the years we've known one another are only the beginning... the future looks bright for us, for love!

To my family, friends and supporters, thank you for the continued inspirations and encouragement. It is very much appreciated!

Dedication: As with everything I do, this novel is dedicated to my children, Dorian Davion and Tamara. I love you with all my heart and I'm so proud of each and every one of you! Never quit, keep striving and keep being great!

To the two women in my life that always see what I never see in myself, who always wants the best for me with no hidden agendas other than their love for me. For the correction and the encouragement, you have been the anchors in my life and I love you more than my heart could ever express. Lanelle M. Jackson & Robin Foster, my sister, my cousin… thank you!

Federal Prison Camp

"Only the Strong Survive"

Charlene looked down at the *Receiving & Discharge* call out sheet, took her freshly Fuchsia polished right index finger nail and skimmed down the sheet of paper for her name. A smile crept across her face as she found her name next to the appointment time of 0700 hours. Finally, she said with a huge sigh of relief, she would be going home. For Charlene it had been a long, grueling four years and six months and now she was ready to put it all behind her as best she could and move on with her life.

There would be some of the 342 women at the camp she would be leaving behind and she would miss tremendously. Those women that had been more like a surrogate family to her during the duration of her sentence, from the Cincinnati county jail, behind the gates of the FCI (Federal Correction Institution), to the camp she was now leaving in the morning. Faces she would never forget and keep in her memory forever. Lessons learned that she would carry with her and use to guide her future, both good and bad.

These friendships were forged under the sometimes harsh circumstances of prison life but they were also some of the realest she had ever been a part of. They way she saw it, in prison Charlene was truly at her lowest. To be trapped inside a 15,000 sq ft box for almost five years, day in and day out was a mental agony that one who has never experienced it, could never understand. All the missed holidays, passing birthdays and the daily simple pleasures that most humans took for granted, such as crossing the street... physically impossible. Yet the women around her knew that pain in some way or another. They understood one another because they too were trapped inside the box of confinement, so she knew that the bonds she had developed with some of the other inmates were genuine.

Unlike street life where everyone tried to out shine one another; in prison they all wore the same blue prison issued khaki suit, the same brand of tennis shoes, the same cheap deodorant and body oil. Yes there were those who had more than the others but for the most part they were all struggling. There was no need to pretend; everyone knew what the other was feeling, everyone knew if your loved ones cared enough to visit you or not, everyone knew if someone on the outside thought enough about you to drop a line and hear your name called at mail call... there was no need for faking... every one's journey was the same in most ways... but there was a few things that could make one's journey stand apart. Some things were unwanted but necessary to keep your journey flowing as easy as possible.

"So you finally leaving huh?" he asked her, smiling as he veered over her left shoulder looking down at the *call out* sheet.

Charlene felt the heat of his breath on her neck and it nauseated her. He by far, would be the one person she would be so glad she never had to see again.

Officer Tucker was a 280 pound, white man with scaly skin like a sunburned lizard. His face was full of pits and deep crates with pores that looked like potholes. His hair was dark black and greasy. You could smell his cheap cologne coming around the corner ten minutes before you ever laid eyes on him. His armpits always reeked of funk and his very messy appearance always put Charlene in the mind of pure-dee trailer trash.

A local Kentucky good ole boy, Officer Tucker was one of Warden Hayes' favorite officers because he always went above and beyond his call of duty to keep the prison grounds safe. He was a stickler for the rules, except the ones he himself or his close co-workers chose to break; those he had no problem over looking.

He was an officer that the inmates in both the camp and the adjoining men's FMC (Federal Medical Center) prison hated to see coming on the day of rotation because they knew that they were in for constant harassment, be it through shakedowns (when an officer goes through every little thing inside a prisoners cell looking for contraband; things the inmates weren't allowed to have), no flexibility of the rules and just the presence of an-all-around asshole on duty.

Each officer rotated for a three month term and most male officers preferred the women's camp over the noise, violence and tight restrictions of the men's facility. The female camp held close to 350 women on any given day and only staffed one guard, one kitchen supervisor and one recreation specialist, two counselors and a camp administrator. With the exception of the second shift guard, all staff was gone no later than seven pm. That left one man on rotation alone to manage three hundred plus women at one time.

The camp was an open camp, meaning there were no bars, no gates and no locked doors to hold the female inmates inside. The inmates were trusted to remain on the compound or pay the consequences of an escape charge which carried a mandatory five years added on to their present sentence and confinement back behind the gates. The camp brought primarily easy shifts for the officers but Officer Tucker liked the rotation at the camp for another reason... power.

He was one of those men who out on the streets probably couldn't get laid unless he came out his pocket for it but on the inside, he knew that there were desperate women, some who had been down (locked up) for as long as twenty years, those who had habits out on the streets and would do anything for a fix on the inside and there were those who played the game of prison life, using their bodies to get what they wanted from the guards. The officers assigned to the camp weren't sent through the same strenuous search process as the guards going inside the main institution, thus they were able to bring in trinkets and treasures to dangle in front of the women in exchange for what they wanted. After all, there were some amazingly beautiful women in prison just as it was out on the streets.

Tucker toyed around with women voluntarily from time to time but the quests that gave him the most pleasure came from the ones he had the joy of breaking down until they complied with his demands. Fantasy girls like Charlene he couldn't even lift his hand to wave at out on the streets.

Charlene was a twenty seven year old mother of two who came to prison after being convicted of drug trafficking; attempting to carry Cocaine on a plane from Ohio to Atlanta. Any crime committed while crossing state lines or in the air makes it an automatic federal offense.

Born and raised by her grandmother in Cincinnati OH, Charlene for the most part stayed out of trouble growing up. Yet, that all seemed to change when she met her children's father Marco at age seventeen.

Marco was a neighborhood dope dealer and Charlene quickly got hooked on the lifestyle he dabbled in front of her and the other chicks in the neighborhood. The money he spent or gave her made her feel as if she was Queen B on the block; the shopping sprees, the designer handbags, clothes and shoes, the diamonds on her neck, ears and fingers, had her head so clouded, she'd do anything to keep him satisfied so that he in turn, would keep her and their children laced with nothing but the best.

She wasn't sure if she loved Marco the man or Marco the money but she dug her nails into him quickly and gave him two children to seal her life with both him and his money. Charlene understood that the game came along with many obstacles; women, safety risks and freedom risks. However never had she imagined it would be *her* doing time, especially while Marco was free out on the streets.

When Marco had asked her to make the trip for him, Charlene didn't hesitate because it wasn't the first, the second nor the tenth time she'd done it for him. This was a part of the game that she accepted as her responsibility for sporting the title of being his lady. She wanted to him to know that he had her loyalty and that she would do anything to keep their growing empire together. That she would take the risk, knowing he'd have her back if anything went down. She would never let another woman get close enough to Marco, his product or their family's lively hood. So this trip she figured was just another routine stop on an itinerary for their family's wealth and fortune.

What Charlene didn't know was that earlier that month, the Feds had put the final touches on a case they were building against Marco's connect in Atlanta and that he was now co-operating with the Feds to pull people in, in exchange for hopefully a lower sentence from the judge.

When Charlene checked into the Delta Airline gate she was a little nervous as always but she knew that Marco had packed the drugs securely around her thighs with tape and wore two pair of leggings in an effort to help smooth the lumps and bumps. She was instructed to place her carry-on bag onto the black roller and asked if she had any containers that held liquid over the allowed weight of three ounces. Charlene answered *no* and watched as her Louis Vat ton bag went through the screening tunnel and cleared security. She breathe a sigh of relief as she took off her shoes, her bracelets and earrings and placed them into the grey container along with her cell phone. If she could manage to clear the final checkpoint, she'd be home free.

When Charlene walked through the metal detector, the under wire in her bra cups made the alarms go off. The awaiting security officer waved the hand held wand across her chest. Charlene hung her head in disbelief that she'd forgotten to put on her sports bra that morning. *How could I be so fuckin' stupid?* She had been arguing with Marco as she dressed, over a text message she'd seen flash across his screen as he taped the dope to her thighs. In the midst of the argument, she'd put on a bra with under wire instead of her sports bra. *Fuck,* she spat out as she stood there, the security guard waving a female officer over for assistance.

11

The male security officer pointed towards the wall and told Charlene to stand off to the side for a personal search. Charlene was then instructed to step inside a screening room followed by a female security agent who proceeded to instruct her to remove all her articles of clothing.

Charlene was wearing a very loose fitting sundress over her double pair of leggings and when instructed to disrobe, she bit down on her bottom lip, her stomach turning in knots as she hesitantly slid the straps from her shoulders one by one and let them fall down to her side. The security agent watched the beads of sweat formed on Charlene's forehead. She knew something was wrong.

The hefty Chinese woman walked closer to her, pressing for her to speed it up. Charlene sighed and obeyed, letting the sundress fall to the floor. The agent shook her head when she realized she'd hit pay dirt. She pushed the button on her shoulder radio. "We got a live one." Immediately she reached behind her back to unlatch her handcuffs and told Charlene to finish undressing.

She complied, exposing the taped bags of cocaine taped to her inner thighs. Charlene hung her head as the agent began to read her rights to her. Charlene had never been in any real trouble with the law and sitting handcuffed to a chair in the Custom's office of Port Columbus Airport, she had no idea what to do nor what to expect.

She sat by helplessly staring in silence as three DEA agents weighed the product on a small digital scale, repackaged it as evidence and then questioned her for over four hours about who she worked for; telling her how she could help herself if she would just co-operate.

Charlene however, refused to answer any of their questions, even after the threats of a possible fifteen year sentence behind bars. She simply couldn't imagine rolling over on the father of her children. She knew the risks when she decided to make the trip and so no, she would bare her own cross. Charlene stood her ground.

12

When she finally reached the Federal Detention Center on East 7th Street and was allowed to make a call, she called Marco. He had already figured that she had gotten pinched because she hadn't called him and told him that she had made it through security as she'd done so many times before.

"You good baby?"

"Yeah, I'm good. They were coming at me pretty hard though but shit, I stood on mines."

"Don't you worry about nothing, you hear me?" he said to her.

Charlene knew that Marco would hire the best attorney for her and he did. By the time she'd made it to court, she knew that her being caught at the airport was no coincidence, bra or not. That's Marco's connect had already set her up. Although it was Marco they were expecting, Charlene's photo was passed on to airport security as well. Her refusal to help them build a case against Marco had pissed off the prosecution.

They returned the favor by requesting the maximum penalty available under the law at her sentencing hearing, even after she pled guilty to *"possession with the intent to distribute."*

Yet, when the judge handed down her six year sentence Charlene was pretty relieved. Yes, it would hurt her to be away from her children and their father but the sentence could have been stiffer, a lot stiffer. The fact that Marco already had two strikes meant that if he had gotten caught, he would've faced life under the three strike law. Once again confirming in her heart that she'd done the right thing by keeping quiet. The low end of her guidelines was five years and the high end was ten years. She indeed had walked away pretty lucky.

Marco had promised to hold her down while she was away and bring their children to see her every other weekend. Charlene felt that with that promise, she would be okay and for the most part she was until about sixteen months ago when Officer Tucker took his much anticipated shift at the camp.

"Be downstairs by the library right after 10pm count. I might as well get one off for the road," he said, poking her against her lower back with his pelvis before walking off.

Charlene despised him and everything he stood for. Everyone knew it was against the law for an officer to sleep with an inmate It was considered *rape* whether an inmate engaged in the act voluntarily or forced because the officer is in a position of authority over the inmate. Some officers refused to risk their jobs on what society deemed the scum of the earth. Officer Tucker however had a fetish and he used his power over the girls, to feed it.

He along with a few of the other officers that abused their power weren't too concerned about getting reported to the warden because no inmate really wanted the label of being a trouble maker on their jacket. Officers, no matter where an inmate transferred to, had the power to make their lives hell on the inside. Charlene's visits and phone calls were all she had and she would lose her mind if they were ever taken away; especially for a slithering snake like Tucker.

As she walked down the hallway and up the back stairs to her room, Charlene decided that her last day on the compound would be one that no one would forget, especially Tucker. She had no choice but to meet him by the library because even with freedom less than 18 hours away, he could still cause her enough trouble to keep her there so yes, she would meet him… but this time she wouldn't be the only one who ended up regretting it.

Chapter Two

Taedra, known to her friends and family as Tae, sat outside with her clear Sony headphones on, inhaling the breeze of the cool autumn air underneath the white metal pavilion on the East side of the Atwood campgrounds. As she leaned back in the silver and blue metal chair, she stared out across the quarter mile long stretch of grass that separated the camp from "true" civilization. The mellow sounds of Jahiem played in her ear as she chilled out under the moon light.

"...all I really want is your Ghetto Luv, 24-7 we'll be making love. I'll take it down that's if you want me too. Just one of many things I wanna do to you. Don't you get scared, I'm gone take my time. Whatever it takes, I've gotta make you mine..."

One of the many privileges of being in the camp as opposed to being behind prison walls was the level of freedom the women had. At the camp the only time they were required to be inside the dorm was the state mandatory count times of four pm, four am and ten pm. Outside of those times, they had the freedom to roam the campgrounds day or night but along with that freedom, came the freedom to make life altering choices.

The Feds believed that the women being held at the camp were of no danger to anyone around them nor the community basically less than 1/4 of a mile away. They didn't have to be supervised at all times and the system trusted them to abide by the rules. Of course 300 plus convicts brought many personalities under one roof and naturally not every woman believed in following the guidelines set forth, especially in such a relaxed environment. Those that chose to buck the system became resourceful in ways you could never imagine.

Tae bobbed her head to the beat and stared out at the cars traveling Southbound on Leestown Road. She slowly inhaled her Black &

Mild cigar, patiently waiting for the pair of headlights to make an appearance on the road that connected the camp to the city streets. This road turned and passed right past the pavilion less than 50 feet from where Tae was sitting, continued down the road that the inmates were allowed to use as an exercising trail, and ended at the parking lot of the twenty-four hour recreation center.

There the officers and their immediate family members were allowed to work out, play ball and hold events. So a car coming down the road at any given hour, day or night, wasn't out of the ordinary to the perimeter guard assigned to circle the camp grounds every fifteen minutes.

Timed perfectly, once the gold Lexus made it down to the parking lot, it would make a quick U-turn, tossing a package in a hidden spot only the inmates knew about. In this package was Tae means of continued survival on her bid.

There was no one family member on the outside that really had the means of putting money on Tae's books on a regular basis. Her mom was on a fixed income and most of the folks she used in her criminal dealings did what little they could do but most had blown through their money. It was only one person she knew had her back and she only asked her for certain favors. Everything else she needed she got through the connections she'd made on the inside or those she left behind in the hood; weed, X pills, jewelry and cell phones were always in demand on the inside. Tae was one of the few who could get it for you without you risking your own freedom.

Everyone had a story before they got to Atwood and Tae was no different. Hailing from Cleveland Ohio, Tae knew early on that she was not the average girl on the block. She knew she was a different breed of female.

Born the baby of two girls, Tae had always known that she was attracted to other girls. She would sit for hours watching her older sister prepare for dates and admiring the beauty she possessed. No, she wasn't attracted to her sister; she was attracted to what she represented; the softness, the sexuality, the seduction and that attraction over the years would intensify.

Her childhood had been a difficult one to adapt to with the overwhelming feelings of confusion she often felt. Naturally her mother, sister and friends expected her to be like normal girls; playing with dolls, jumping rope and things like that. Coming up, Tae rejected anything *girlish* and instead she spent her time playing ball with the neighborhood boys, skate boarding, and playing tackle football, any activities that helped her to embrace who she felt she truly was deep inside. She kept her hair braided in the freshest styles, she stayed in baggy clothing and sweat suits constantly to the dissatisfaction of her mother... to Tae, dresses were kryptonite.

Tae's mother didn't like the fact that she was so boyish in her ways; hoping somehow it was just a phase her baby girl was going through and that like her sister before her, Tae would grow to prepare herself to one day be a wife and mother. To her father however, it just became normal and he had no quarrels about Tae's tomboyish ways; having no sons, he and Tae shared a lot of things in common such as sports, fixing cars and grinding.

One of the many reasons Tae was so cool with a lot the guys in the neighborhood because she was very skilled on the basketball court. Earning several high school and college honors as well as three trips to the state championship, she could handle the rock just as good any male opponent she faced. Her game landed her a spot on the *Cleveland Crush* Women's Semi-Pro Basketball Team as a starting point guard for two seasons until she tore her ACL in her 3rd year off season training camp.

Now out of the league, she still needed to survive. The league had brought her a certain status in the community that Tae felt she needed to keep up, by any means necessary. Tae began to nickel and dime her way into the dope game, selling ten dollar capsules of Heroin out of one of the neighborhood trap houses. She was one of the smartest hustler's on the block taking the game she learned from her father and she quickly put her name on the map.

By twenty-seven, she was on top, enjoying the fruits of her labor while others hustled for her. She had come into her own as both a hustler and a fully fledged lesbian.

Tae was considered "butch" by term but she was attractive to many, both women and men. The women flocked to her because she had it goin' on, in some ways more than a man... She had the street credibility, the money, the cars, the house... all the things that made a man a hot commodity but Tae's gender to some was a plus. Women often felt that dating a "stud" was in a way, the best of both worlds. They could also provide for you like a man but understood you better as a woman, therefore could treat you better because they knew exactly what you like, how you liked to feel and what you needed to be complete.

Unfortunately Tae, like many other studs, did just as much dirt as men, if not more, simply because it wasn't expected of her. She played around with many, liked few but loved only one... Kelly, Tae's fantasy woman. Kelly was tall, her body thick as bricks, with slightly pimpled chocolate skin, medium length burgundy colored hair, a good job, a nice car and most importantly standing on her own two feet.

Working as a medical assistant, Kelly was different from the many women that Tae ran across, always looking for a hand or a step up without being willing to work for it. Kelly didn't need someone to take care of her, she dated because she wanted to and that indeed was one of the many things Tae found so attractive about her; that plus the fact that Kelly wasn't into the gay life meaning she had never been with a woman before. The challenge that presented made Tae want her all the more.

Needless to say, it boosted a stud's ego to turn out a heterosexual woman (get a woman who only deals with men to cross over and experience her side of sexuality) and to Tae, Kelly was the ultimate quest. When Tae first laid eyes on her pumping gas at the local BP, she literally began to drool. Standing there in spaghetti strapped silver dress that stopped right above her thighs, Kelly was breathtaking. Tae had always been a very outspoken woman. She had the level of confidence that whether a woman turned down her advances or not, she would always take the opportunity to let it be known what was on her mind with no regrets. In her eyes, it could end only two ways, the female could either get in the game or stay on the side lines. Tae's self esteem was way too high to let a no stop her flow, so she shot her jumper whenever and wherever, without hesitation.

She walked over, took the gas pump from Kelly's hand and finished pumping her gas for her.

"A woman as fine as you are has absolutely no business pumping her own gas."

Kelly smiled and looked at Tae standing in front of her dressed in all black Polo shorts and top, the top opened just enough to expose a set of well defined abs. Tae loved the fact that she had flat chest because most studs, tried to hide their breasts, some going as far as to use an Ace bandage to smash them down. Tae on the other hand was able to simply wear a sports bra underneath her tops and nothing else. Her abs were ripped like a pro athlete.

Draping from her neckline was a gold chain with a diamond encrusted cross. Tae's wrist was laced with a gold and diamond bracelet and her fingers sported a few rings.

Kelly looked down to Tae's extended hand and chuckled slightly. She figured she'd be cordial since Tae had taken the time to both say hello and finish pumping her gas. Yet when their hands touched, Kelly like the softness she felt. Tae took her thumb and

19

slid it back and forth across the back side of Kelly's hand. She didn't know quite how to respond as Tae began to spit her rap in grand form. And while the words coming from Tae's mouth sounded all too familiar to Kelly, the sound in which they came across was different.

Sure, Kelly had thought about experimenting with a woman before, mainly in her late high school/early college years but the opportunity had never really presented itself. And while she knew it wasn't a lifestyle she'd be comfortable enough to flaunt in public, in private she acknowledged the curiosity of a woman's touch. A curiosity of what a woman could do for her sexually and how it could differ from that of a man. She would never vocalize this curiosity but it played a major part in why she gave Tae her phone number.

Chapter Three

Melody bent over on her Bunkie's lower steel bunk bed in pain, gripping the white cotton blanket so tightly inside her hands. Beads of sweat poured down her forehead as she clinched her abdomen in agony. She didn't know exactly what was wrong but she knew whatever it was, it was drastic. Melody had never felt pain like she felt at that moment. She bit down on her pillow trying to muffle her screams. She knew one thing though, something had to give and quick.

Nationwide standing 4pm count would be happening shortly and she could barely move. Unless you had a slip from the medical unit, every inmate was required to stand during count, no excuse. As she lay there, she tried her best to gather herself. Melody, known on the compound as Mel, couldn't believe the things she'd experienced over the 30 months she'd been locked down. What started out as a breezy lay down had somehow turned into a nightmare.

Mel was woman enough to admit that she'd played a major role in her current situation and that a lot of her trials had come at her own hands and her own decisions. Somehow, she'd simply allowed it all to get out of control and over take her.

What had started out as a simple game of sexual flirtations had somehow ended with the destruction of so many lives... how had she allowed it to come to this? Had her insecurities from the past truly blinded her sense of judgment?

When Officer Terrance Connors first walked onto the Atwood Compound, it was only his second assignment. He was young, dark smooth skin, low cut waves in his hair, a sexy athletic physic and although he had braces on his teeth, his smile was simply gorgeous. Yes he was hot and being a rookie; less than ninety days out the academy, he was unprepared for 300 plus women, volleying at every turn for his attention.

Shift Rotation change is never announced ahead of time and you never know which officer the camp would pull until you saw them at 4pm count. Mel's senses instantly came alive as she could smell him before she actually laid eyes on him. The intoxicating smell of his cologne told her whoever he was; he wasn't one of the regular guards. Most of the male guards that rotated at the camp wore cheap, knock off versions of cologne but whoever this was coming down the hallway, keys jingling, footsteps heavy, had taste... good taste.

During count time no one was allowed to move or talk or be prepared to face write up. The smell of him however drew Mel to the doorway as she stole a quick glance at the 5'6; slightly bow legged, handsome guard coming her way. When he approached the door way to count her and her roommate Chell, Mel waved at him and he in return nodded his head in *hello* as not to mess up his count.

From the moment she'd laid eyes on him, Mel knew she had to have a piece of him... knew she would do anything to get him. At the time she still had seventeen months left on her sentence and seeing him every day would definitely make the time pass.

Mel was one of the prettiest women on the camp grounds; flawless coffee brown skin, long natural hair and nails. She was small in height with the body of a video vixen. One she'd known how to use to her advantage. Unlike most of the inmates at Atwood, Mel's commissary stayed stacked and her books financially plush. From a variety of sources, the cash constantly flowed in... mostly from a few of the older guys she'd left behind on the streets.

Mel had decided from the moment she'd caught her case that whatever time the judge handed down to her, she would be well taken care of. She believed in preparation. She was smart enough to know that once the Feds had you, they had you and it's a war you could fight but one you're guaranteed to lose.

So when Mel's on again-off again dad hired a high powered lawyer to get her bail reduced and had gotten her released, she set a plan in motion. She played nice with a couple of upscale men from "*PT's*," the strip club she worked at, formed alliances with prior girlfriends so once her sentence was announced, her bank account looked very attractive.

When Mel turned herself into the Atwood camp on June 3, 2006, phase two of her plan began… security. Women could tell once you settled in on the compound if you had money. Mel knew that just like on the outside, everyone wanted to be on the team of a winner and while all the inmates wore the same scrubs, uniforms and jogging suits, it was the small things, things those often took for granted on the outside that set you apart from the other inmates. Anything that you had to pay for with commissary or by putting money on someone's books… manicures, pedicures, liquor, drugs, jewelry, perfume and even certain nail polish were luxuries only the elite inmates could afford.

It was also the high end things sold on commissary. The average inmate made $14.00 a month from working a 40 hour work week. At roughly $.12 an hour, if you didn't have outside help, you had to learn to survive on that and that alone. So there was no way that you were purchasing the finer things on the commissary list.

For example, the commissary sold two pair of shoes, the average basic Reebok running shoe and a rotating variety of Nike/K-Swiss. The elite inmates sported the Nikes'/K-Swiss or outside sneakers. Inmates, who were allowed to turn themselves into the compound of their own free will such as Mel, were afforded the opportunity to bring in their own sneakers.

Mel had done her research as to what the inmates was allowed to have in their possession on the compound. Items such as jewelry, shoes, etc. Before she hit the highway to Kentucky, she stopped at Lee's Pawn and Jewelry on Martin Luther King Blvd., to buy herself a 14kt gold chain with a gold and diamond cross pendant, three pair of gold hoop earrings all different sizes, a gold bracelet, watch and a solid wedding band.

These were the allowed jewelry items on the compound but of course those sold through the chaplain's office where made of cheaper gold and were very plain. Mel as always wanted to stand out.

So in order to get her new purchases onto the grounds undetected, she had to stash it and smuggle it inside. There was only one way to do that. Once she made it to Lexington, KY, she pulled over at the Phillips 66 down the street from the compound, went into the station and asked the big elderly clerk for the key to the rest room. She bought a few small items such as donuts and chips in order to get a plastic bag.

Inside the restroom she emptied the bag into the sink, bit down on the plastic to tear it, placed her jewelry in the bag and tightly tied it into a knot. She reached down inside her purse and grabs the small jar of Vaseline as she sat down on the commode and spread her legs as far apart as she could get them. She took a huge scoop of Vaseline and saturated the bag with it, wiping the remainder of oil on the lips of her vagina. She inhaled a deep breath and released it forcefully as she shoved the bag inside her and pushed it up into her vagina cavity as far as she could. She used her fingers to maneuver the bag until she felt it poke against the right side of her cervix. Then she took a wad of tissue, rolled it up like a tampon and placed it up inside her opening as well.

It was always so risky to try and to smuggle anything onto prison grounds inside your cavities because of its natural moistness. There was no guarantee it would stay in place as every inmate were forced to "*SSSC,*" (strip, squat, spread 'em and cough) as a part of the intake process. Anything illegal was considered contraband and guaranteed you a trip to county lockdown and possibly another charge added on before you ever stepped foot onto the compound.

When the Receiving Officer told Mel to "*SSSC*," Mel prayed the Vaseline she used wouldn't come back to bite her in the butt. The tissue was also there as a second line of defense. So that if the guard saw anything it would be the whiteness of the tissue and Mel could try and justify it by saying she was on her period and was wearing a tampon. She let out two deep coughs and she could literally feel the package pushing against the opening of her vagina threatening to burst through.

She'd never felt so relieved when the officer told her to "dress out" and threw her light blue scrubs to her. What she couldn't take on the compound, was packed and shipped back home to her mother. What she could, was rolled up and given to her.

In order to the leave Receiving and Discharge you had to walk the outside grounds that ran alongside the rec yard of the adjoining male FMC (Federal Medical Center) and wait for the shuttle to drive you over to the camp. When she walked out the gate, she could hear the men yelling and whistling to her from inside the fence and as always, Mel liked the attention and once she noticed just how close their facility was to the camp grounds, she knew she'd soon have a little fun.

The men however would have to wait though, she frowned. Her first order of business was to relieve the throbbing pain between her legs, one that seem to worsen the more she walked. She had pushed it downward from its resting place when she coughed and it was now pressing down against the sensitive flesh of her vagina opening.

When Mel entered the white freshly painted steel door of the camp, she looked around at the busy scene. The women were moving about back and forth from the cafeteria which was directly in front of her, where lunch was being served. The big glass windows soon filled with faces; women rising from the grey metal tables, looking and wondering who the new inmate arrival was.

25

Often women wanted to see if they knew a new inmate from their hometown or had they served time with her at one of the other federal facilities. New inmates were also a hot commodity... most women were looking out for someone new to hang out with.

Her face may have seemed familiar to a few of the inmates from their home town, especially if they had frequented the strip club. Mel was greeted by one of the elder inmates as she stood in the middle of the floor looking around. Ella had been in the system for over eleven years when Mel met her. Locked up for a charge of conspiracy, Ella had refused to snitch on her son and because she had made a few phone calls on his behalf to his drug counterparts, the Feds rewarded her with a sentence of 240 months... twenty years. Ella directed Mel to the Officer's station to check in.

"Thank you ma'am," Mel told her as she entered the small office. Once she was assigned her dorm room, she immediately went to the dorm style shower and jumped in. As the hot water beamed down on her back, Mel squatted down and began to push slowly as she used her fingers to reach up inside her vagina cavity and retrieve the plastic bag. As she navigated the bag, she saw the drips of blood fall onto the shower floor. The roughness of the package had scraped against her inside walls.

Small thing to a giant, she told herself. First impressions were often the best impressions to Mel and as she washed the blood from her hands and the bag she retrieved, she was ready to turn the compound out. She was stuck for 3 years; she would make the best of it... Mel's way.

Charlene took the back stairway to her room on the second floor. Eyes watering, she had had enough. Nothing would give her more pleasure than to rip his penis off and shred if for all the mental torture he had caused her over the past eighteen months. She already had so much going on the outside, things that had threatened to dismantle her sanity.

By any means necessary she needed to get home to get her children. Charlene had spent four Christmas, Thanksgivings, Mother's Day and Birthday's away from her children. In the Feds you got 54 days of good time taken off your sentence every year as long as you didn't get into any trouble, plus six months of time at the Half Way House. So on a six year bid, Charlene was heading out in 4 ½. While each year seeming a little easier than the previous one, it scared Charlene because she was always afraid of getting to comfortable away from home. She felt as if that made it seem as if she was okay without her son and daughter. That was by far the furthest thing from the truth.

Things had noticeably begun to change over the past four years with Marco, her children's father. When she first began her bid, Marco kept his promise and faithfully bought their children to see her twice a month. Then he began to slow, saying it was becoming too expensive to keep traveling. Charlene understood that because Marco had been forced to get a job by his PO from a misdemeanor drug offense he'd caught a year into her serving her sentence and she tried not to complain but not only did the frequency of the visits change, the letters all but stopped. Her phone calls were answered far and few in between. Without her mother, Charlene would've hardly ever been able to lay eyes on her children the last two years of her bid. It was also her mother who made sure Charlene was kept up to speed on the children's progress.

Marco on the other hand had become a master at excuses; he was always working overtime or he couldn't get away because his PO hadn't approved his travel form. Yet it was something told to her by her seven year old daughter at their last visit that told Charlene that his absence had less to do with work and more to do with a woman.

Charlene was devastated. She couldn't believe that the man she loved, the man she believed in, the man she was serving time for would betray her this way. Yes, she knew he would fuck other women while she was away; to think any other way was insane but it was an unspoken rule… you fuck, you don't get involved. You definitely don't have the trick around their kids.

Later that evening Charlene used her phone time to call Marco. She knew what her daughter Kayla had told her, had substance by the way Marco had been so evasive in answering her questions.

"Why you coming at me with some shit Kayla told you? This a fuckin' seven year old and you gon' listen to somethin' she tell you? Yo', you be straight on one," he told her as he put his finger up to his mouth, gesturing for his female companion to keep quiet. "I'm out here trying' to keep shit afloat for me and *our* kids. You know I ain't out there like that no more. I gotta pull shit together through a legal gig. Shit ain't that muthafuckin' simple no more. So if I gotta blow through one of these bitches out here, to make sure yo' kids good, what's the big fuckin' deal?
Help comes where it comes, feel me?"

Charlene wiped her tears as she listened to Marco's words. She had no choice other than to accept them but they stung like hell. Ultimately she understood that he needed help with the kids beyond what her aging mother was able to supply. When she was out on the streets, she hadn't made many friends due to the arrogance in her personality. The few women she did hang around, only put up with her antics in order to enjoy the fruits of Marco's labor in the game. So basically, Marco and her mom was literally all she had to rely on when it came to care of her kids.

"Yeah Marco, I feel you."

"Well quit callin' me with this bullshit. That's why I don't answer half the time. Between yo' letters accusing me all the time and phone calls like this, you drivin' me crazy. Lena, you in there, I'm out here, what you want me to do?"

"We had a deal Marco, I do this time and you do it with me. You move but don't move on. It just seems to me that for the last few months you been sliding away more and more. No letters, visits slowing down and all you do is remind me that I'm in here as if I don't know that."

"Look Lena, I don't have time for this shit, I'm at work," he said, unbuckling his black Lee jeans. "I gotta go, my boss callin' me. Aey, I love you Lena," he told her, hanging up the phone.

Charlene looked down at the receiver in disbelief.

"Yeah, I love you too," she whimpered, returning the phone to its cradle.

She held it together as best she could as she passed the other women in the phone room and those waiting outside in the hallway. When females saw you crying, the side show always began with insincere questions, *Are you ok? Bad news from home? You wanna talk?*

Charlene knew that all it was were some nosey females trying to get in her business to have something to spread later. So she held it together until she was inside the back hallway alone before she felt a slew of tears began to fall from her eyes.

When Officer Tucker came down the back steps, he encountered Charlene at the door. He noticed she was crying.

"You alright," he asked her, handing her his handkerchief from his uniform shirt pocket.

Charlene told him she would be okay.

"Just bullshit at home, ya know?"

"Hey just because I go home everyday don't mean there ain't bullshit going on there too," he said putting his hand on her shoulder. "Come on to the office and tell me about it, I may just have some insight and advice for you."

It wasn't unusual for an officer to sit and talk to the women at the camp. Often for the women, there was no one else they could trust. Even the counselors gossiped about inmates and their business with other inmates and staff. So Charlene really didn't think too much of his suggestion.

"I'm always an objective ear."

She followed Tucker to the office, took a seat and began telling him her story as he peeked out the door to see if anyone was wandering the hallway before closing the office door. As she talked, Tucker stood behind her, rubbing her shoulders. Charlene felt uncomfortable by his touch but appreciated an ear to listen and provide her some perspective as a man.

"You should know how this works by now dear. Pussy is just that, pussy. However your loved ones have to survive out there, you gotta suck that shit up. You made the choices that landed you in here, not them, so you can't be mad at what you left them to deal with, right?"

Charlene felt his hand squeezing tighter against her skin.

"We have to do things sometimes that we don't wanna do; that's just a fact of life. Wouldn't you agree," he told her. Sliding his right hand down her shoulder of her grey t-shirt to her breast.

Charlene swallowed the lump in her throat.

"Yeah, I... I guess so. Well, thank you for listening Officer Tucker," she said, squirming away from his touch. "I really appreciate it. I'm a little tired so I'm gonna head on up to my room and shower before count."

Charlene began to walk towards the door.

"Well now Inmate Sheppard, you won't be going anywhere until I'm done with you. Have a seat," he told her, pointing to the chair.

Charlene slowly walked over to the chair, swallowed the lump in her throat and looked up at him pleading with her eyes. Most of the inmate/guard relationships at the camp were voluntary but there were the few, the few like Officer Tucker, who took pride in the power of force-able persuasion.

Tucker shoved her back into the chair with his left hand as he unzipped his dark grey uniform pants zipper with his right.

"I been watching you for quite awhile. I just knew there come a time when the opportunity would present itself. It always does with you little whores in here. Ya'll layup, let another woman suck on ya pussy's before taking some real dick," he said pulling his penis from his boxers.

"Well now, here's some real dick, show me what you can do with that," he said, grabbing the top of her head and pulling it towards the pink five inch-worm.

Charlene felt the tears roll down her face. She had heard of stories like this but she herself had never been in this position before.

31

When she didn't move fast enough, Tucker yanked at her hair and forced her to rotate her neck.

"And I know you nigger gals know how to suck dick better than this… teeth-less and without choking, so act like it.

Charlene held her breath, trying dull her senses of smell and taste. He smelled horribly and the bitter taste coming from off his penis told Charlene he hadn't washed that day and maybe not the day before. It almost made her throw up. She tried to take her mind to another place, somewhere where the thrusts he made inside her mouth didn't exist.

She tried to think of Marco while holding her breath until she was on the brink of passing out. She felt him swell inside her mouth and when she tried to pull away he grabbed the back of her head and held it as he began to fill her mouth with his disgrace.

"Swallow it!" Swallow all of it. I don't want a drop of evidence in yo' mouth, hear me… swallow!" he yelled as his body began to spasm from release.

Charlene became light headed but knew that the only way he was going to release her was for her to swallow the tart venom from the snake that had issued it.

Tucker backed away from her and told her that if she ever wanted to get home and see the nigger she was crying over or her kids again, she'd better keep quiet.

"You and I both know I have the means to make it happen, Understand?"

Charlene told him yes and after he ordered her to open her mouth so he could check it, he walked over and opened the door, looked out to make sure the coast was clear and released her. Charlene darted up the steps to the second floor bathroom, into a stall and repeatedly stuck her finger down her throat until she threw up all the contents of her stomach. She cried as she hurled over the toilet, thinking to herself, how she didn't sign up for this.

The day she decided not to co-operate with the Feds had come back to haunt her in ways unimaginable... and someone was going to pay for that... someone other than her.

When Taedra reached the Federal holdover facility in Oklahoma, she thought of Kelly as she leaned back against the dingy beige concrete wall of the holding main cell. From day one Kelly had stood beside her; from arrest, bond hearings, lawyer maneuvers, trial and ultimately sentencing.

Tae had become Kelly's world and the things she'd experienced from her relationship with her, she simply wasn't ready to let go; it wasn't even an option for her. Tae closed her eyes and thought back to the first time she'd made love to Kelly.

She had begun the evening, making reservations at one of Cleveland's premiere eating spots. She spoiled Kelly at every opportunity that presented itself. Buying her purses, clothing, and jewelry and leaving money in places she knew Kelly would eventually have to look so she'd find it.

Kelly adored the way Tae doted on her, not only for the material things but she loved the way Tae showered her with compliments, always noticing every little changing detail about her; new hair style, eyebrows arched, nail polish change, new jeans, etc. To Kelly, it spoke volumes. It let her know that Tae was truly into her.

Wherever they went, Tae always made it known to the world that Kelly had her heart and her full attention. That is what ultimately sent Kelly head first over the cliff for her. While she had strong feelings for Tae though, Kelly wasn't too quick to engage in a sexual relationship with her. It wasn't that she wasn't attracted to her; in fact Kelly got turned on at the mere sight of Tae. Whether it was watching her play ball on the local courts, working out or simply pulling up to pick her up from work.

Truth was Kelly was afraid because while she was feeling Tae, she didn't know if what she felt towards her was simply a passing phase or if she could truly remain in it for the long haul. Tae was

34

so good to her and the last thing she wanted to do was hurt her. She had been so patient and so understanding of her feelings. Kelly just needed to be sure that what was between them was permanent and while her heart told her so, in her mind, all she could hear was her mother telling her how what she was doing was so wrong in the eyes of the Lord.

Kelly also thought of her sexual inexperience when it came to being with a woman. If it were to happen, Kelly wanted to be able to please Tae as well, without inhibitions. After months of soul searching, Kelly decided that she was ready to go to the next level with Tae. She didn't quite know how to tell her, so she decided to go for it.

They were celebrating Kelly's new promotion at the medical center when they arrived at *Giovanni's Resturaunte*, an Italian spot on Chagrin Blvd. Tae had no clue that Kelly had spent the day planning her own special little surprise. She'd gotten off work early that afternoon and headed to the mall.

First she stopped in *Bath & Body Works* to pick up some scented candles. Then she went to *Fredericks of Hollywood* to find the perfect outfit that screamed, *come get this pussy*; a perfect little red and black laced teddy with matching garter.

She set the mood before Tae picked her up for dinner… candles, music, rose petals, scented body oil and chocolate covered strawberries chilling in the fridge. The music selections que'd and ready to go with the simple push of a button. All she needed to do was separate herself from Tae after dinner to give herself a little finalizing time.

This worked perfectly for Tae because she had already committed to a previous business meeting that she couldn't postpone and she didn't know how Kelly would take it, calling it early on such a special occasion. Tae had slowly accomplished putting down the drug life but replaced it by picking up a Western Union money order scam with one of the young ladies she'd dealt with in the dope game.

Donna worked as a loan processor in a check cashing place with access to unlimited packs of blank money orders. She would use unsuspecting employee's codes to cash the money orders that she'd given to Tae, who in turn brought in people with fake IDs. Donna would get 40%, Tae would get 40% and the one cashing the money order would get 20%.

It wasn't hard finding some crack head to be a willing participant in exchange for a small treat. Tae did the hard work, setting them up with the IDs; all they had to do was stand at the window, avoiding the cameras as best they could, sign them and cash them. For the big jobs though, Tae used some of her closest family members and in return, she put a nice amount of cash in their pockets. It normally took about 90 days for authorities to catch the transactions in the system and by that time, the fiends were long gone.

That night she was supposed to meet up with Donna to get another stack of money orders. So when Kelly told her that she wasn't feeling well and she needed to go home, Tae was kinda relieved because she hated lying to Kelly and Kelly had no clue of what Tae was into on the streets. She knew Tae hustled but not to that extent. Tae kept her clueless to the depth of her illegal activities in order to keep her shielded from any potential legal fallout.

When they pulled up in front of Kelly's apartment on Brook Park Road, Tae told her that she'd be right back within' the hour.

"I gotta handle somethin' right quick and then I'll be right back to take care of you. You need anything?"

"Just you, be back soon."

"You never have to ask me twice." Tae answered, leaning in to kiss her.

"Here," Kelly told her, placing her key in Tae's hand. "I may be lying down when you return. Let yo 'self in."

Tae watched to make sure that Kelly got in safely before pulling off. She took out her BlackBerry and called Donna to let her know she was on her way. When she arrived at Ace Cash Express on East 55th street, she pulled her Platinum colored Range Rover up onto the parking lot next to Donna's cobalt blue Dodge Intrepid. Normally Donna would get out and get into Tae's passenger side but tonight for some odd reason, she waved Tae over to her car instead. It kinda caught Tae off guard for a second but once she saw that Donna was sitting there rolling a blunt, she quickly dismissed the thought. Tae got in and closed the door. Donna immediately began asking her all kinds of off-the-wall questions.

"So how many more people you think we can bring into the mix by next month. I'm planning a trip to Vegas and I'm really tryin' to do it up, feel me? I got somebody that wanna be down wit' us too so, I need to know where you be getting' them ID joints."

Tae lit up the blunt Donna handed her and asked her what was up with all the questions.

"I'm sayin' bitch can a muthafucka get a hello or somethin' first? You actin' like *Hawaii 5-0* or somethin',"

"You got me fucked up, you know better than to come at me like that Tae. I just told you I'm tryin' to get to Vegas niggah, make moves and make money," she said, reaching behind her seat and grabbing the stack of money orders. "Plus the new chick that wanna get down sayin' she want the same cut we getting. She can bring mad clientele but I told her that forty percent just ain't gon happen, so if we double up on the amount of money orders we do, we can all break bread. Listen Tae, this," she said, placing the

37

stack on money orders on Tae's leg. "Ain't gone keep getting us where we need to be much longer. Big bosses are crackin' down, so that's another reason we need to get as many cashed as we can, as fast as we can and get out."

Tae's intuition told her that something just wasn't sitting right but against her better judgment she decided not to question it. Whatever it was, she told herself, would make its way to light soon enough. As she inhaled the blunt all she could think about was getting back to Kelly.

"Aight, we'll reconvene in the morning. No worries, you know I'm a make it do what it need to do. I gotta bounce right now but real talk, I'll fuck wit' you in the AM," she said, getting out of the car.

Tae took the stack of money orders and placed them down underneath the driver's seat of the Rover. She'd have to leave them there until the morning because she didn't want to make anymore stops that night; that would come back to haunt her but that night, all she wanted was Kelly.

As she drove along the side of the East Bank, she cruised to the sounds of Res' For Who You Are. *"...you were my lover, used to be my best friend, someone I really loved to talk to when my day was coming to an end. I know we had to grow apart but I never knew things would get so hard... and I'll always love you, for who you are....."*

Kelly had taken allot lately to be with her and Tae recognized that. Kelly's mother, a minister was truly broken hearted over Kelly's choice to commit what she described as the "ultimate blasphemy" in God's eyes. They were at the point that they were barely speaking and Tae knew that deep inside, that crushed Kelly. Yet she made Tae feel like their growing relationship was the only thing that mattered to her and for that Tae would always give her the world or die trying.

So when she turned the key to Kelly's apartment and opened the door, she had all intentions of showering her with the love she felt for her.

What she got was a sensual surprise when she found Kelly standing in the middle of the living room, fragrance candles lit all around, rose petals lining the floor... their path leading to the heels of the red stilettos at the bottom of Kelly's long beautiful legs.

Standing there, one hand on her hip, the other sliding down her diamond belly piercing, she looked gorgeous. The red and black lace teddy fit her perfectly; from the snuggling around her thighs, the lifting of her 36C breasts to the rim of her ass cheeks hanging underneath.

Tae's mouth watered at the sight before her. She closed the door, dropped the keys on the floor where she stood and walked over to Kelly.

"You look amazing Bae," she told her, looking around the room. She spun Kelly around so she could take in the full sight of her. "You feelin' some kinda way?"

Kelly leaned in and ran her tongue across Tae's bottom lip.

"Can't you tell?"

She took Tae by the hand and led her to the bathroom door.

"Shower... and hurry," she told her, opening the door and exposing the candle lit bathroom with more white rose petals thrown across the lavender rug.

Tae stepped inside, undressed and as she turned on the shower, she thought back to Donna's words, *"Vegas... and I'm going to do it big."*

As she slid her jeans down her thighs, she couldn't help but smile. No woman had ever gone through so much trouble to make her feel special and it felt good, real good. So good, that mimicking Donna's idea of getting away, she thought that it would be a great idea to take Kelly somewhere nice on a trip. Her hustling was bringing in some pretty good dough, so why shouldn't they be able to get away and relax?

She stepped into the glass framed shower and let the hot water run down her back. Again something Donna said popped into her head. How the money order scam would only get them so far. *Maybe it's time to leave all this shit alone and just roll legit*, she thought to herself; maybe go back to college and finish her degree. Yes, she loved spoiling Kelly and the streets made it so easy to do that but Tae was no longer sure if she wanted to risk the life they were building together. She wanted to be right for Kelly, so at that moment she made the decision that once she'd gotten rid of the stack she had, she was done.

She stepped out of the bathroom and entered the living room. Kelly was standing beside a chair in the middle of the living room floor. Kelly directed her to come over and sit down. Tae smiled a devilish grin and quickly obeyed. She took a seat as Kelly picked up the remote from the smoky gray glass table and hit play.

Out over the airways came Genuine's, *So Anxious*. Kelly walked over to the kitchen counter top, grabbed the baby oil along with the chocolate covered strawberries and placed them onto the table next to the remote. She took the belt off the arm of the grey and black couch and walked back over to Tae.

"Hands behind your back."

Tae's eyes perked and a naughty smirk came across her face. She tied Tae's hands with the pink string and slowly strutted around to the front of her chair and began to grind her hips seductively.

"...I'm so anxious; meet me at 11:30. I love the way we talkin' dirty, said I'm so anxious, girl can we get this started you know I'm a sex-a-hol-lic..."

Kelly rolled her hips as she ran her hands across her breasts, squeezing her nipples and licking out her tongue. She sat down on Tae's lap, thrust her upper body forward towards the floor, popped her ass up in the air and moved it cheek-by-cheek. She bounced up and down on Tae's thighs and Tae's mommy began to throb between her legs. Hands tied, she was helpless to touch and feel the beautiful mound of thickness before her and it excited her beyond measure.

Kelly stood up, reached over to the table, grabbed a strawberry, and lifted her leg resting her heel on Tae's thigh, placed the strawberry into the opening of her mommy then bringing it up to her lips, bringing her tongue out to greet it before inserting it into mouth. The sight of her tasting her own juices drove Tae crazy and she wanted so bad to get free and participate. Kelly grabbed the baby oil, lifted it above her upper body, threw her head back and squeezed the clear liquid all over her chest. She removed the straps of her teddy from her shoulders and rubbed the baby oil into her breasts. She continued to move the teddy down her abdomen and let it slide down her legs to the floor as she picked up the oil once again. Her back to Tae, Kelly poured the oil down her back and let it run down her ass cheeks.

She bent forward, rubbed the oils into her cheeks before she placed a hand on each cheeks, pulled them apart to expose her mommy. She ran her hands down her calves and back up to her thighs, smearing the glistening oil across each one. She began to play with her mommy as Tae squirmed harder to get loose. Slowly she placed her fingers inside and began to finger fuck herself to the sound of the beat. Tae was losing it.

"... Said as soon as I hit the door, I'm a throw you down on the floor and before we get to touch the bed, baby back up every word you said..."

Kelly had one hand on the floor and the other inside her, gyrating her hips and ass.

"... Baby girl I wanna bump and grind, this is somethin' that's been on my mind, so anxious..."

Tae couldn't take it, she jumped up as the chair fell to the floor and she hurried over to Kelly.

"Untie me baby, please... now... can you please... untie me."

Kelly loosened Tae's hands and instantly became engulfed by her touch; her hands going wild across Kelly's body. Rubbing, touching, squeezing, and gripping every inch of her skin; Tae kissed her from head to toe. Slowly she teased her nipples, down to her stomach before pulling her down onto the floor full of rose petals.

Tenderly she nibbled on Kelly's calves, slid her tongue up the inside of her thighs. She paused however to make sure that this was truly what Kelly wanted. She wanted her to have absolutely no regrets.

"We don't have too Bae; we can stop right now," she told her huffing and puffing. "If you want it, you gotta say it... tell me... say it... say it!"

Kelly answered by grabbing Tae at the back of her head and pulling it back to her mommy.

"Take me Bae; take me to your world."

Tae stood up, pulled her up to her feet and told her to go lay down in the bed.

"I gotta grab something real quick from the truck."

"Now?" she squirmed.

"Trust me baby, it's for u."

Tae ran down the steps, over to her truck, grabbed the bag out the back compartment and paused for a minute. She had the strangest feeling that someone was watching her. She looked around, didn't see anyone and jetted back up the steps.

She went into the bathroom and removed the 9in flesh like strap-on from inside the bag. She stepped inside the laces, tightened them around her thighs and waist, and then placed the suction cup over her clit.

Tae walked into the bedroom to find Kelly sitting in the middle of the bed, body glistening from the oil in candle light. When Kelly saw the strap on hanging between Tae's legs her eyes widened.

The touch of Tae's tongue across her shoulder blade made her tingle. Tae explored Kelly's body again, this time making a long pit stop between her thighs. She widened her mouth, wrapped her lips around Kelly's mommy and her clit at the same time; softly sucking on the flesh between her teeth. She rolled her tongue across her clit and Kelly felt a sensation she had never felt before. Yes, she'd experienced oral sex with men but Tae kissed her mommy with the same passion and admiration as she'd always kissed her mouth with.

Gently she took her teeth and clinched the mound of sensitive mass as she locked her arms around Kelly's thighs. She flicked her tongue across the top of it and Kelly began to scream. She dug her nails in Tae's arms as her body began to spasm.

Tae rose up and took a moment to tower above her, staring at the almost innocent look on her face. She spread Kelly's legs apart and Kelly reached up and tried to touch Tae's breast.

"Nah nah Bae, I don't need all that. I don't like it. My only pleasure comes from seeing you pleased, feel me?"

She lay back and allowed Tae to love her completely. From slow wine to getting flat out assaulted by the strap on, Tae took her to heights of pleasure previously unknown to her.

Tae wanted her heart, she wanted her soul and she wanted her loyalty for life and she knew how to get it.

She lay down on the floor, propped her feet onto the mattress and instructed Kelly to stand over her, squatting with her legs spread apart. Tae inserted the toy inside her and began to thrust upward with a vengeance. Kelly felt a tension build that felt like her bladder was about to burst; growing with each stroke. She couldn't handle what she felt, afraid she was going to lace Tae with a waterfall of golden flow. She jumped off the toy, gripped the mattress with both hands and she screamed as she felt her clit pulsate and watched in amazement as her mommy began to squirt out liquid; springing from her vulva, all over Tae's chest. She jumped back onto the bed, grabbing her clit and rocking side to side, mumbling insanely to herself.

Tae climbed beside her as she panted and tried to help her slow her breathing. Kelly panted as she lay in Tae's arms. She had just experienced something amazing and she had no idea how to stop the electricity shooting throughout her body as a result. She snuggled close to Tae all that night, loving every minute of her on a whole new level. Tae had made love to her two more times during the night and Kelly knew that in Tae's arms was where she wanted to remain, no matter the cost…. That was until a knock came at the door the morning after.

Mel learned the way of the compound pretty quickly. The first lesson she learned was to keep the details of her case to herself. The only one who knew why she was in the system was her counselor, Ms. Garnet.

Ms. Garnet was the campus' ghetto version of *Wendy Williams.* She was always in some body's business and she kept up with the campus' gossip as if it was her daily soap opera.

She was in charge of assigning the inmates jobs, so if you played her game or became one of her flunkies, you could end up on one of the crews that actual was able to work off the camp grounds in the nearby city of Lexington. Likewise, if you got on her bad side, you were guaranteed to pull one of the worse jobs at the camp, clean up detail or the mess hall.

When Ms. Garnet looked at Mel's file, she frowned up her face and looked up to her. With a strong distaste in her mouth, she asked Mel what could have possibly been going through her mind the day she caught her case.

"Don't look like it was much at all. I mean who transports dope on a plane inside of a dead baby? Really, who does that shit? That shit just sounds insane."

Mel looked at the judgmental old battle axe and frowned.

Who the fuck are you to judge me? You don't know me, she thought to herself. *You don't know my story.*

Mel had grown up in the Pruitt Igoe Projects of St. Louis, MO. The oldest of four kids, Mel learned at an early age the power of what her body could do for her.

Budding out as she attended Stevenson Middle School, her breasts, thighs and butt took on the shape of an 18 year old young woman. It wasn't her former 8th graders that had noticed her expanding frame but rather her older cousins that her mother left in charge of her and her younger brothers and sisters. One cousin in particular... his name, Brian.

Mel's mother worked at one of the local city buildings by day but fed her cocaine habit at night. It seemed sometimes that she only worked to supply her addiction as opposed to taking care of home and her children. Many of nights they went hungry, the lights turned off every few months, the clothes on their backs used and poor Goodwill quality.

Her cousin Brian was a construction worker and made pretty good money. Single with no kids, he also made money on the side selling a little weed to his friends. Brian would bring them something to eat as well as drop a few dollars in Mel's pocket since she was the oldest and also since he stashed his drugs there.

One day while visiting, Brian placed a one hundred dollar bill on the brown coffee table in front of her. Mel, at twelve years old, had never held that much money in her hands before and her eyes lit up at the sight of it.

"This Mines?"

"Yeah baby girl, it can be. As a matter of fact, you can have way more than that if you do a few small things for me," he told her, sitting down next to her on the green and purple flowered couch and placing his hand on her arm.

"What you want?"

Mel expected him to ask her to wash some clothes, clean his shoes, iron... things she already did for him from time to time but she definitely wasn't prepared for what he said next as he moved his hand to her lower thighs.

"You growing up Mel. You ain't no little girl no more, at least not by the way yo' body is developing. Now life is hard out here and I know you tired of not having nothing. I bring you crumbs but if you get on board with what I have in mind for you, you can get the whole slice of bread. Niggah's I know will pay you nicely to touch that body of yours and even more to fuck you. Good money too, you hear me?"

Mel looked at him and then down to the money in her hand. She returned it to the coffee table and shook her head.

"I don't want none of yo' friends touchin' on me. That's nasty."

"What's so nasty about it? What's nasty is this damn apartment. Look at this shit. Look here baby girl, you wanna keep on living like this? You wanna keep wondering if yo' mom care enough to bring her ass home at night to feed ya'll? If you gone make it to school every day because you gotta stay here and babysit, losing out on yo' education? You can get up out of here if you want and I can help you. Just stack the money you make and when it's time, make yo' move.

I know you love yo' lil brother and sisters so I know you might not wanna leave them," he said, rubbing her on the shoulder.

He slid his finger underneath the strap of her halter top and pulled it down her arm.

"You don't have to leave 'em. You'll have money to feed 'em when they hungry. Don't you want that?"

Mel looked at her youngest brother sleeping on the pallet she'd made him on the floor. She had to put him to sleep with a bottle of sugar water because her mom hadn't brought home milk, again.

Yes, she wanted to take care of her siblings but did it really have to be like this? With her body? Was this truly the only way?

Mel's dad was a high priced business accountant that had literally disappeared once he remarried and had more children. He never came around anymore. She might get an occasional call or some money when he bothered to remember her birthday.

She had no aunts on her mother's side, only an uncle who was doing time. Now here was his son, telling Mel she needed to sell some pussy in order to survive.

"How many?" she whispered to herself. "How many would I have to let touch me?"

She picked back up the money and stuffed it into the back pocket of her faded blue jean shorts.

"Well, you know I'm a protect you right? I always look out for you, that's not gon change," he said, rubbing his hands on her budding breasts. "You a virgin so I ain't gone let none of them nigga's break you in. That should be reserved for someone you know. I'll tell you what," he said, peeling off another fifty dollar bill from the wad of cash he had in his shirt pocket. "You take this and add it to the other dollar I gave you.

I'll be the one to break you in cause I know I'll be gentle like it's supposed to be done. I ain't gone hurt you. You know that right," he said, standing up and pulling Mel up to him. "Now you gone and put the kids in yo' momma room and make sure you lock the door behind you and come back in here."

From that day on, Mel made a living with what she had, not what she thought nor what she knew. She serviced clients throughout her high school years with Brian alongside her. She only focused on two things, her siblings and her money; they were the only two things that came to matter to her. Mel never got the pleasure of

48

knowing high school games, dances, proms, skip days… nothing. She did what she felt she had to do to keep her and her siblings okay.

That all changed when her mother got so high one afternoon she cooked some food for her youngest brother in a pot she'd used to cook up her dope, mixing enough residue in his food that he ended up having to be rushed to the hospital. This brought DFS (Division of Family Services) deep into their business and the three youngest kids were removed from the home. Mel however was seventeen and allowed to stay with Brian.

The only way she had a shot at getting them back was by getting her mother crack free. That would take an expensive treatment facility and money, a lot of it. So when one of her clients propositioned her with the idea of transporting drugs, Mel saw an opportunity to help her mother get well, get her siblings home and pay for her cosmetology school. She had begun working at the strip club for extra money and was hoping to be able to let it go as well.

The many short trips she made at first were easy. Her partner in crime worked at the city morgue and when the babies came through the morgue, after autopsy but before going to the funeral homes, he would steal the bodies, stuff them with drugs and book Mel's flight.

Short flights raised no suspicions. Mel looked like the average young mother traveling with her baby. On the short flights, no one bothered to notice why the baby didn't cry; make noise or why she never fed the baby on board. Once she returned, he simply returned the baby to the morgue and called the funeral home for release of the body. No one would suspect a thing.

This flight however would be different, it possessed a challenge. While it would bring her triple the amount of pay, it would be a five hour flight and Mel was visibly nervous, rightfully so. She'd have to pull off a perfect act. No newborn went five hours without making a sound and no matter how great Mel's effort was to keep up the charades, the flight attendant wasn't fooled.

The slender perky white female stopped the meal cart next to Mel's seat. Mel was holding the corpse as if she was sleeping on her chest. The attendant asked a visibly shaken Mel if she could place the baby's bottle in the compartment refrigerator for her because the flight still had over two hours to be in the air.

Mel, trying to go along with the plan said yes. The problem came when Mel had to shift the corpse in order to grab the bottles from the diaper bag planted between her feet below the seat. The attendant watched closely as the baby didn't move, squirm nor make a sound.

She pretended all was good until she alerted the Captain who in turn alerted the authorities in Dallas. When she stepped off the plane, she was greeted by Federal DEA agents who took the corps from her arms and cuffed her.

Mel was given a lighter sentence because she chose to co-operate. She continued the journey to deliver the drugs to their destination, got the money and then returned back to St. Louis, all under the watchful eye of the DEA.

She couldn't afford a lengthy sentence. She had to get back to her brother and sisters. So no matter what she had to do to get there, it was going to be done.

She'd learned the day Brian took her virginity that everything and anything someone wanted or expected of her came with a price. She helped the DEA make their case against her co-conspirators and she testified at their trials. In exchange, they dropped off eight years off her sentence and kept her close to home so she could see her siblings whenever their mother was able to bring them.

Mel's earlier flights had helped her mother successfully complete a residential treatment program and regain custody of her siblings.

"Survival," she answered,

"What?"

"You asked me what I could've possibly been thinkin' when I caught my case... survival."

"Yeah well if you ask me, I think it was some pretty sick ass shit. I mean how you gone sit and hold a dead baby for five hours both ways on a flight?"

"Hmm, I don't know but thank God I didn't ask you what you thought. Can I have my job assignment now please?"

Ms. Garnett frowned and rolled her eyes.

"You might wanna watch yo' smart ass mouth. You startin' off wrong already. Don't get wrote up on yo' first day. Mess Hall," she said, throwing the paper on her desk.

Mel snickered as she grabbed the paper and headed out the office,

"Ole Bitch," she mumbled as she bounced down the steps.

Mel showered, dressed and pulled her long hair into a pony tail. She put on a few items of jewelry and as she walked past the inmates in the hallway, all eyes fell on her and she loved it.

She had to get her detail signed off by her supervisor and when he laid eyes on Mel his lust was clearly visible. He signed Mel's slip and asked her if she'd eaten.

"No thanks, I ate before I turned myself in. So when do I report," she asked him, straightening her clothes and throwing a loose string of hair from her face. "I hope it's not too early because I am so not a morning person."

"Since it's your first day, I'll put you on the late shift so I can train you myself," he said, winking his eye at her.

"Thank you," she told him, flashing a smile. She had already gotten her way in less than two hours on the compound. Yes it was a small thing but as Mel knew all too well, with the right motivation, small things often led to bigger things.

As she stood in the shower scrubbing her face in an attempt to scrape away every ounce of his disgrace, Charlene thought back to Kayla's words, *"She fixes my hair for school every morning Mommy.... every morning."*

Yes, Kayla was only eight years old but Charlene knew that what her daughter was trying to tell her was true. That this woman, whom Kayla called Ms. Tiffany, was more than just a fuck to Marco.

How could he do me like this, she cried. I could've gone a whole different way if I'd known you were gonna fuck me over like this.

In prison where phone calls are limited, sometimes your mind had a way of finishing a conversation for you... filling in blanks that weren't even left open. Thoughts run rampant, whether rational or irrational and if you didn't get a hold of them quickly, they could take you places that didn't sell round trip tickets, meaning you couldn't come back from it.

I could've walked away from this with nothin' but probation. But nooo, I had to be the loyal bitch, the ride-or-die. I fell for the bullshit, hook-line-and-sinka! How could you?

Charlene didn't know which was destroying her more, Marco's betrayal or Tucker's assault. Both were weighing heavily on her soul as she continued to try and wash his smell from her face.

After ten pm count, Charlene headed back to the phone room. There was no way she could sleep without clearing the air with Marco. She needed answers and she needed the truth, no matter how bad it would make her feel, she just wanted him to keep it real.

When the other end answered, she heard what she'd thought was Kayla's voice on the line but when the prison recording stopped and the voice returned she knew better.

"Marco's in the shower, Is there anything specific you'd like for me to tell him?" the female voice asked her.

"Who is this," Charlene asked.

"This is Tiffany, his girlfriend," she said matter-of-factly.

Charlene had her answer. Marco had lied to her.

"Are my children there?" Charlene asked, swallowing the pit in her stomach and trying to keep her composure.

"They're asleep. Kayla had an upset stomach so I gave her some meds and rubbed it 'til she drifted off. If you like I can…"

Click

Charlene hung up, she had to because she had no idea what could've flown out of her mouth next. She was angry, so angry. How could he have another woman in the home with her children, rubbing her daughter's tummy? Missing holidays was one thing but moments like this, no one in the world could understand unless you'd been there.

She quickly walked out the phone room before she burst into tears again. She ran up the back stairs to her room, placed her robe over the small square window so no one would disturb her, flopped down on her bed and let it out. The thought of her family being cared for by another woman was a hard pill to swallow.

Charlene's roommate Nikki walked into the room and sat down beside her.

"Bunkie, what's wrong honey? Are you okay?"

Nikki, a forty-two-year-old woman, convicted of shooting her husband in the face was serving a twenty three year sentence. Her crime was federal because she lived on a military base. Her husband Shawn, an Airman, had a nasty habit of taking his day out on Nikki, good or bad.

The good days were rewarded with beast mode fucking, slaps on the ass and the bad, slaps to her face. The night she was arrested, Nikki had taken a routine beating from Shawn. When the MP's made him leave the home, Nikki took a pain pill and fell asleep on the sofa.

When she heard the locks on her door being tampered with she grabbed her husband's gun from underneath the couch, rolled onto her back and began firing. She told the CID officers (Criminal Investigation Division) that she thought he was an intruder and when she heard the noise at the door, she just fired. She might have walked away from the incident uncharged had she not told the officers that the sound she had heard, were keys jingling in the door lock.

To the DA, that told him that she knew it was her husband and she fired at him intentionally. Nikki started her journey in Maximum security for two years, then to the FCI for nine years and now here she was at the camp for her final six years. Any violent crime committed on the Federal level required 85% of time served, no exceptions, so Nikki couldn't earn good time.

With not much to lose, Nikki had a "*fuck it*" attitude. She did as she pleased when she pleased. Long timers were well respected on the grounds, not only for their reputations but their wisdom on how to do time without letting the time do you.

They taught the young newcomers how to leave the outside exactly where it was, outside.

"Marco has another bitch in the house wit' my kids."

"And?"

"What you mean and? We had a deal when I took this case, no prolonged bitches; stick and move only."

Nikki chuckled.

"Girl if you don't sound stupid. What niggah you know finna sit at home while his baby momma doin' a six year bid, jackin' his dick every night? I mean seriously, you expect a man raising two kids under ten to handle that all by himself? Lena you can't fuckin' be serious right now?"

"I get the fact he gotta fuck, I do. I even get the fact that he need some help caring for the kids but shouldn't no bitch be rubbing my baby's stomach ache away!"

"Bitch is you crazy," Nikki said, lying down beside her. "The problem for me would be him havin' a hoe around that wouldn't. Just sit there and let my baby hurt. Look Lena there's something you need to understand and the sooner you do, the easier yo' time gone be. You fucked up, not him, not the kids. You! And you can't expect er'body's life to stop cause you fucked up. That man still gotta live while you here.

Don't be one of these dumb ass bitches walkin' round here in fantasy land cause when reality welcomes they asses home, they ain't gone know how to deal wit' it. Fuck wit' reality now so you're equipped to handle *whatever* is waiting for you out there, feel me?

Marco ain't hold no gun to yo' head and make you put that shit on you. *You* chose that role. So in reality, Marco don't owe you shit, Lena. Yeah you'd like his loyalty but niggah's don't think like we

56

do. They preach loyalty all day but you had to have known that he wasn't gone hold out for long. You had too. At least be good with the fact he found a bitch that's woman enough to care enough about yo' kids to rub a tummy. Could be worse.

Now yo' kids got a roof over their heads, food, clothes and somebody to look after them. You ain't there, not yet. So until you can get there, be thankful they aight cause we both know it's a lot of women in here that don't even get to have contact with their kids.

And how you know he ain't just using that bitch 'til you get out? You ever thought of that?" she asked, sitting up. "You know how that shit goes Lena."

"Then why not just be real with me and say that?"

"Probably cause he knew yo' ass was gone act exactly the way you acting right now."

They both chuckled and for a moment Charlene felt a little better. She knew Nikki was telling her the truth, real and raw; just what she needed to hear.

"Let that man live his life girl. When you get close to your out date, then you see what's up, 'til then keep everything mellow. The last thing you wanna do is push him to the point the visits stop and the money stalls. Shit bitch every letter you write oughta start off with, 'thank you baby for being the man you are' or some shit like that. Make that niggah feel like he dat deal.

You need him on yo' side 'til you out that gate. You don't wanna give her no more power than she already got, so you keep his thoughts of you nice and sweet. Let him know that pussy throbbing for his touch, stroke that ego. Give him something to look forward to when you get out. Matter of fact, use that road.

Hell you know how niggah's think and ain't nobody had that gushy shit... trust he gone straighten up right before it's time for that tight shit to hit that gate."

They both laughed as Nikki stood up to reach down inside her pillow for a late night treat.

"Come on outside with me. Get yo' mind off that shit," she said, holding up a joint. "Let's blow one."

Charlene rolled off the bed and stood up, fixing her grey sweats.

"Thanks Nikki," she said, hugging her. "You knew exactly what to say."

"Hey you don't sit in these four walls without learning something over the years."

Charlene leaned back against the steel railing of the bed and sighed as she looked off to the wall.

"What do you think about Officer Tucker?"

Nikki stepped back and looked at Charlene for a moment and then shook her head.

"You too huh? Damn... yeah, you need this high. Come on," she said, putting her arm on Charlene's shoulder. "One question though before we hit this joint?"

"What?"

"Did you brush?"

"Fuck you," Charlene said, pushing Nikki out the door.

As she waited for the delivery of her package, Tae thought back to the first day she hit the compound and the day she'd met the girl who would change her world.

When she left the holding facility in OK, all she could think about was how she couldn't wait to reach her destination, get settled in and have Kelly come to visit. She missed her more than she imagined she ever could. Kelly had made an imprint on her life and Tae felt so incomplete. She thought that by being surrounded on a ward of 150 plus women, she'd think of home a little less often. Although she mingled and flirted with a few, she quickly realized however that without Kelly, this time away could turn out to be a very hard pill to swallow.

She had come to love her so much. It was something about knowing she was Kelly's first and only female relationship that made her love for her stronger. Through all the ups and downs they had experienced with Kelly's mother feeling the way she did concerning their relationship, Kelly had stood tall and showed loyalty and that drew Tae closer and closer.

Still being the woman she was, Tae knew that dealing harmlessly with a woman on the inside here or there would make the time move a little faster. As they led all the traveling inmates out the steel metal doors to a line of awaiting transport vans, Tae was shackled at the ankles to a gorgeous twenty three year old convicted of bank robbery in Tennessee.

Shelby, known as Bright Eyes because of her beautiful hazel eyes was small framed, thin waist with an ass to die for, firm looking thighs and a nice set of D cup breasts that had Tae's mouth crooked at the corners. Even with her un-permed hair matted to her head, Tae was infatuated with her beauty.

"I couldn't have asked to be shackled to a finer woman," she told her, touching a mole on her left pinkie finger. They were also shackled around their waists with each of their wrists cuffed to each side of their body and to the waist chain.

"Is that so?" Bright Eyes responded, smiling and shaking her head at Tae.

She too admired the creature standing next to her as well. Tae had her hair freshly braided by one of the other women at the facility. Inmates traveled in the street clothes they wore to court so Tae was dressed in a black pair of slacks, a long sleeve white shirt with a purple, grey, black and white paisley tie. She had on a black belt and a pair of Stacy Adams shoes. She looked very nice and Bright Eyes along with many others took notice.

Along the van ride to the airport, they engaged in good conversation about where they were from, their charges, their sentences and where they were headed. They soon found out they were headed to the same place… Lexington, KY.

"What the fuck a pretty muthafucka like you doin' robbin' a bank? You been watchin' too much *Set It Off*?

That got Bright Eyes to laugh. She loved a person with a sense of humor.

Hailing from Nashville, Bright Eyes was a well educated young girl who decided early she would do exactly what she pleased with her life, no matter who objected. She ran with the wrong crowd often to the dismay of her parents. She belonged to a local street gang of Bloods and the leader had been her boyfriend for the past six years.

Bright Eyes came from a very well to do family and even though she basically had everything at her fingertips, the excitement of the hood life and the wrong side of the law seemed so much better to her than the stuffy life of the suburbs. Bright Eyes visited her cousins every summer in the city's Andrew Jackson projects, where she met Antonio A.K.A Tone.

Opposites definitely attracted as Bright Eyes found a missing sense of importance being announced around the hood as Tone's main girl. She loved being on display on his arm, especially since he was a very attractive man himself and a lot of women volleyed for his attention.

Tone was a thief. It was all he and his crew did to survive. It wasn't the benefits of his lifestyle that drew her in; she could get anything she wanted from her parents. It was his commanding ways, his cockiness and his roughness that attracted her.

Tone's crime spree was able to last so long because he often went to the outer cities to do his dirt which meant that by the time the local news aired news of the robbery, they were long gone on the highway.

Tone never asked Bright Eyes to join in on any of his criminal adventures. In fact she begged him to go along the day they were arrested. Tone had been casing a bank in the neighboring city of Clarksville, TN for the past several days and he was ready to move in. The only problem was that the Feds had gotten an anonymous tip telling them the next spot Tone and his crew had planned to hit so they were ready when Tone and company entered Regions Bank. Any bank that is federally insured is federal property making it a federal offense.

Normally Tone only used notes that threatened the clerk saying he had a weapon but strangely enough the day they ran into Regions and the Feds drew down on them, Bright Eyes found herself in the middle of a gun battle which ended in Tone killing a federal agent.

Bright Eyes was officially charged with Capital Murder since the agent died during the commission of another felony but once they learned that it was her first ride along, her first arrest and Tone assured them that she had no idea he was armed, the Feds dropped the charges down to 2nd Robbery and Bright Eyes took the plea deal for 48 months.

With time already served, good time and halfway house time, she would only have a little more than fifteen months left to serve. Her parents refused to bail her out because they were tired of her getting into trouble and this time she had simply gone too far behind Antonio. After this charge was resolved through sentencing, her father wrote her a letter explaining his position. He would not visit, nor write any further, nor send any money past the check for fifteen hundred dollars he had included, a one hundred dollar a month stiffen. He had washed his hands of his daughter but did explain to her that if she changed her life while in prison that upon her release they could sit down and talk.

Bright Eyes shed no tears. She totally understood why her father felt the way he felt. They had worked their butts off to lay the world at her and her sibling's feet and how did she repay them? With a felony record. She understood that from that point on, she was basically on her own doing this time. She no longer had Tone. He was doing life and now with her family turning their backs, Bright Eyes knew she had to fight this battle alone. That fact, unbeknown to Tae made her dependent, very dependent.

"Damn Bonnie, that's what up? That shit kinda fuckin' sexy to me. Holdin' down Clyde and shit. Well since you basically short timin', how about lettin' me brighten up some of them cloudy days for you... *Bright Eyes*," she teased.

Back and forth they talked of Tone and Kelly, their families and the road ahead. The van came to a halt at the air strip and they were ready to board Con-Air, in inmate plane. Holding four hundred seats, Con-Air was built for heavy protective transport. Designed specifically for transporting prisoners of all custody levels from low to maximum, on board you'd find metal cages at the back, metal railings in the floors and ceilings and each side of the seats. Each prisoner was shackled to the floor and the sides of their seats and if you had to stand, the ceiling. The only time they were not cuffed was to eat.

"Damn, if this muthafucka go down, we fucked," Tae said, trying to move her feet around. "How the hell we supposed to get outta here?"

"Don't worry, I won't let you drown," Bright Eyes told her.

That made Tae smile. By the time the musty smelling plane landed, Tae and Bright Eyes were well acquainted. As they stepped off the plane, Tae's eyes bucked. She had never seen anything like it in her life. Surrounding the plane was roughly two hundred US Marshals, shot guns aimed at them as they came down the steps. K9's were barking and ready to take a bite out of anyone that looked like they wanted to run.

Tae, Bright Eyes and seven other women were walked to an awaiting van while the men who were going to the Lexington FMC was put on a bus behind them. The remaining inmates remained on the plane to continue onto their destinations.

As Tae rode down the Lexington streets, she scoped out the set up of the property. Tae knew she was going to bend a few rules so she paid close attention to the surrounding area.

"Pretty open huh?" Bright Eyes remarked.

"Looks perfect to me," Tae replied as the van pulled onto the parking lot of the men's facility. The nine women were ushered inside the main gate of the male facility and then un-cuffed and directed to an awaiting Receiving Officer. Once processed the van took the women to the compound and when Tae walked inside the front door, Bright Eyes instantly knew that keeping Tae's attention was going to be a challenge.

It seemed as if the world stood still as the women eye fucked Tae from the moment she'd stepped inside. Tae on the other hand loved the attention and had to admit that she'd had a few *eyegasms* herself. The women at the camp were looking much different than the women at the transfer center. These women's hair was done, were dressed nicely, smelling good and many of them looking good. Tae saw a buffet of booties and Bright Eyes tried her best to keep Tae's eyes focused on her and her alone.

"Maybe we could see if we can room together," she said, nudging Tae on the arm.

Tae looked at her and smiled.

"Yeah that would definitely be nice seein' you fresh out the shower, nothin' but a towel on everyday ain't bad... ain't bad at all," she said, eyes following a Spanish inmate walking by and winking at her.

Bright Eyes knew she'd better come correct and quick or Tae was about to slip through her fingers just as quickly as she fell into them.

"Lotta scattered ass around to see huh? I'm wondering if maybe you wanna wash some of this plane dirt off... together."

The suggestion made Tae's eyes perk up and gave Bright Eyes her full attention, if only for the moment.

"Fuck yeah, you ain't gotta ask me twice. But uhh.... it's gone have to be a lil later momma, I got a call to make first."

"Kelly?"

"No other," Tae told her, winking at her and touching her chin with her finger tip. "Don't worry, I got you."

"You're new here, so if you need some things to shower with I can hook you up," Shawna, a lifer suggested to Tae extending her hand.

Tae looked up at the tall thin white girl twirling her finger in her red curly hair; her freckled face red from blushing. Bright Eyes looked down to Shawna's hand, up to Tae and back down to Shana's hand which Tae was now holding.

"Umm excuse me; don't you think that was a little rude? You don't see me standing here? You didn't think to offer me some soap? I mean damn, my pussy funky too right now," Bright Eyes said, trying to offhandedly suggest to Shawna she was entering shark filled waters.

Shawna however didn't even respond, she kept her eyes on Tae and watched Tae's reaction to what Bright Eyes had said. To her, that would let her know if Tae was involved with Bright Eyes on a level that gave her a right to interrupt their conversation.

"Thank you; ugh ... I'd really appreciate that. That's very sweet of you."

Shawna smiled at Bright Eyes.

"Awesome, after you get checked in, I'm in room #126 just around the corner here to the left," she told Tae, pointing down the hallway. "See ya then. Oh and my neighbor Anitra is cold with braids; I'm sure she'll hook you up whenever you need it. Not that you need it. I mean you're already hot but she can make you burn," she said winking at Tae before turning to walk away.

Tae chuckled and wiped the corners of her mouth,

"You don't say? Burn huh? Well like Usher said, gotta let it burn," she laughed.

This was definitely going to be an entertaining stay she told herself.

"Little Red Riding Hoe," Bright Eyes said sucking her teeth. "I see these bitches gone be a hot fuckin' mess. How she gonna come stand *right* in front of my face, don't speak and then offer you some soap and not me? Who does that?"

Tae found it a little cute that Bright Eyes was showing a little jealousy.

"It's all gravy baby, we showering together remember? We can share the lather... I'll make sure that thang get nice and clean."

Bright Eyes smiled as Tae's name got called from the Officer's station. She leaned back against the wall and spoke to a few of the women that had passed her. She wanted Tae, she didn't want to do this time alone and she had no plans too. With her family practically non-existent in her life since sentencing and Tone's letters coming two to three weeks apart, she told herself that Tae was going to be hers, no matter what she had to do to make that happen.

When Tae came out from the officer's station she told Bright Eyes she had to go holla at her counselor Ms. Crumple down the hall.

"She should let me make this call," she told Bright Eyes while looking down at the commissary sheet the officer had just given her.

Bright Eyes saw an opportunity to get a jump start on all the vultures she knew would be offering to get Tae things in hopes of Tae taking a liking to them.

"We can handle this later, we can just put it all on mine and I'll make sure you get what you need," she said, taking the long

66

printed sheet from Tae's hand. "I'm saying, it's the least I can do since you cleaning the funk off me and shit."

Tae nodded her head and smiled.

"I see you, that's what's up. I like that in you baby. I love a lady that knows how to handle her business."

Bright Eyes looked Tae up and down as she walked past her to the officer's station. Tae watched her ass bounce to the jiggle of her stride. She couldn't wait to put her hands on it. First thing first though, she needed to call home and check in with Kelly. Tae knew she had to keep Kelly's mind focused on them and her spirits up. With her mom constantly in her ear, Tae knew that with every passing day and her absence growing, Kelly was vulnerable.

When Tae walked into the small cluttered office of Valerie Crumple, a sixteen year veteran of the prison system, she was greeted and told to sit down. Ms. Crumple began to go through Tae's file, reading her PSI (Pre-Sentencing Investigative Report, which detailed the inmate's childhood, any past criminal history, education, Psyche evaluations and any other information deemed relevant to the inmate's life before committing the crime they were subsequently convicted of).

Ms. Crumple noticed that Tae went to college but never completed her education, played sports at the semi-pro level and that her psyche profile showed she had a very dominant personality. These were a few of the things she used to find the inmates jobs she felt they could excel in once their mandatory sixty days were up in the mess hall.

"I'm assigning you to Recreation. You've got the background and the leadership capability."

Ms. Crumple also noticed the classification notes highlighted in Tae's file. She looked at Tae over the rim of her Gucci glasses and began popping the ink pen in her hands against the desk.

"I know right now this may seem like a smorgasbord to you but let me be the first to warn you. Not every woman in this place is mentally capable of handling the type of relationships you may be tempted to indulge in. Outside of the fact that homosexual relationships are against the rules, we're not stupid so we know it happens. But it comes with allot of bullshit and drama. Some can handle it, most can't. I don't know which one you are but you might wanna remember that when choosing which forbidden apple to pluck from the tree, understand?"

Tae nodded her head as she signed the paperwork Ms. Crumple placed in front of her.

"Ion't make no noise Ms. Crumple. I ain't new to this, it's what I do. It's how I live. Speakin' of, can I make a call home?"

When Tae heard Kelly's voice come through the receiver, she almost melted. Ms. Crumple pretended to be doing some work on the computer but she was really ear hustling the conversation. If it was one thing she knew, was that regardless of how good they had it at home, being away eventually made inmates make some costly decisions that usually landed them back in her office, begging for transfers to other institutions, room assignment changes or loss of out dates due to fighting.

"I miss you so much baby," Kelly told her, sitting in her car on the parking lot of the Beachwood Family Health Center where she worked. "I hate being without you. Are you ok? When can I come see you?"

Tae reassured her that everything was OK and that she too was going crazy without her. She told Kelly that she was in her counselor's office setting up for to her visit as soon as possible.

"I know what you thinking Bae. I know all the thoughts that's bouncing around in yo' head. You ain't gotta worry about none of that. You just stay focused, I got me. Can't nobody hold a candle to you, feel me? It's all about you baby and I'ma hold you down just like I know you holdin' me down, aight?"

Ms. Crumple chuckled to herself. How many times had she heard that? Not just from the lesbian women but also from women telling their husbands the exact same thing only to end up in same sex relationships on the compound. Yet she had to admit, she hadn't heard put quite as smooth before.

When Tae hung up the phone, she grabbed the papers from the desk, handed Ms. Crumple back the telephone and stood up to leave. When she reached the door Ms. Crumple called after her.

"With all that bullshit you just spit on the phone, you gone be a mess runnin' around here; I see it coming. Just don't let me catch you slippin' Ms. Adams, do you *feel* me?"

"Like wool covers on a hundred degree night and the A/C broke."

Connors walked up the back 2E stairwell on his way to finish up his rounds on the second floor. This was the final week of his opening rotation at the camp and he had to admit, it had been a very interesting three months.

Filled with various flirtations, innuendos, notes left on his desk filled with all the things the sender's would love to do to him, for him and with him. In his own way Connors teased them back, making sure that every day he came on the compound for work he looked good, he smelled good and he greeted as well as treated each and every woman with genuine respect.

He didn't talk down to anyone, he didn't ask about their cases or personal business, he gave them general conversation and a non-judgmental ear to listen if needed. He was liked... and well desired. While surrounded eight hours a day by several beautiful women, one had caught his eyes since the day of his rotation.

When he'd passed by her room that first day, she'd given him a wave *hello*. Even while trying to maintain the focus of the task at hand which counting the inmates with a fellow officer... he noticed her.

Yes, he'd passed several rooms that day, saw several pretty faces, nice bodies and such but this one's face was different. For a reason he couldn't explain, she had caught his attention over all the other women.

Unlike those who chose to leave secret notes of want and desires for him, this one took a different approach to getting his attention and letting him know that she had her eyes on him as well.

Seductive gestures that teased his senses. She'd come into the office asking for the simplest things looking like a supermodel, smelling good, hair done, makeup flawless and body always showing in the half cut after hour attire she'd made from her uniforms.

She was bolder than the others, unafraid to say what was on her mind or better yet, show it. Connors had been a rotation for a little over two months and he made his way up to the second floor, he flashed his light inside each room, checking for any signs of what the camp deemed as *inappropriate* behavior. Not much that could go on by camp rules be considered all that inappropriate by his standards.

As with any man, had he walked upon to walked upon two women engaging in a sexual act, he definitely wouldn't write it up... watch maybe... but not write it up. As he approached 204E, he flashed his light down at the bottom bunk to find an inmate asleep with her back to him. When he lifted the flashlight he also found the inmate to be asleep or at least pretending to be. It wasn't so much that she was asleep got his attention but more so the position in which she lay that stopped him dead in his tracks.

Their bunk beds were up against the wall to the left of him, their heads up towards the wall in front of him, so as she lay with her body on her stomach, her ass was facing him. There the creature lay uncovered, legs spread apart with her right knee pulled towards her chest, exposing her panti-less mommy to him. She peeked out at him through the small slits in her eyes before pretending to become restless and shift her body over onto her back.

Connors stood there, looking over his shoulder before returning his eyes and light back to the now full view of her mommy.

Mel spread her legs wide as she could, reached down with her left hand and spread her vagina lips apart. Slowly she began to play with the moist flesh between her fingers. Connors felt his jimmy grow against the inside of his left thigh. Mel took her right hand and inserted her two middle fingers inside the pink opening

71

between her thighs. It turned her on tremendously that he watching, wanting her and his jimmy responding.

The juices on her fingers glistened in the light of his flashlight and he tried his best not to enter the room and go over to her bed. The temptation played such a cruel joke on him and his jimmy began to throb against his leg. He decided that he needed to stay safe so he just shook his head and walked away. He couldn't risk someone coming out into the hallway and catching him.

Mel smiled to herself knowing that she'd definitely put something on his mind and that no matter what, she'd be a part of his thoughts that night for sure. She rolled over with no need to complete the job. She knew that she would have the opportunity one day, soon.

Connors moved down the hall shaking his leg trying to return his size large jimmy back to its correct resting place. He tried to shake the thoughts of what he'd just witnessed but he couldn't shake it. Not that nor the next two days. Thoughts of the creature played in his head, in his dreams and his fantasies; causing him to jack off to the persuasive desires of touching her.

The night before his rotation ended, Mel had come up with a plan for him to get a better view of her, more up close and personal. She wouldn't allow his rotation to end without him at least touching her essence.

Upon his rounds, Mel knew he'd be coming by, possibly hoping to get a another glance of the peep show she performed for him previously but when he flashed his light into her room, he found her bunk empty. Mel however had left him a clue as to her whereabouts. Connor's looked at the small box of *Tide* on the top of the locker and proceeded to continue rounds to the other side of the building where the laundry room was located.

Mel was listening for the sounds of jingling keys in anticipation. As she heard him approaching she hopped up onto one of the white

72

GE washers, unlatched her white cotton bathrobe, flinging both sides open, exposing her naked flesh. She leaned back against the coolness of the washer, reached to the side of her and turned the small white knob to *spin*. As the machine began its cycle, Mel placed her right heel up onto the ledge of the window.

Connors, right on cue, entered the entrance of the doorway, light in hand. He paused at the creature, looked behind himself to ensure the coast was clear then proceeded to enter the dark moon lit room.

"I knew you'd come," she told him, nodding for him to close the door behind him.

The laundry room was the in the middle of the hallway on each floor, a small room holding two washers and two dryers and the only room on the compound that could lock from the inside if you knew what you were doing.

Mel instructed Connors to take the step ladder from behind the door, place the handle underneath the door knob and put the legs up against the bottom of the dryer. With entry now blocked she waved him over to her.

"Been thinking about you," she told him, reaching down on the other side of her, picking up the cool crisp object from the window sill.

Mel had gotten a slender but nice sized *cucumber* from the kitchen at work earlier that day. Often used as a substitute dildo, Mel had placed a latex glove over the hardness of the vegetable and tied a knot at the base to secure it.

Connors walked over to her in amazement. He'd seen a lot of things but this one was new to him. He stood in front o the washer staring down at the sight in front of him.

"God you're beautiful," he told her, wanting so badly to touch her but afraid of what could happen if he did.

He stood there, watching as Mel toyed around at the opening of her mommy with the handmade toy. She lifted her fool from the washer and placed it on Connors' chest as she inserted the vegetation inside her.

Soft moans of pleasure escaped her lips and sent chills down his spine.

"I know you want to but you're afraid. Afraid of how good this pussy might feel. It's all good; you don't have to, not now. But you can still join in. Take your dick out, let me see it. I know that its big, I saw the print the night you were in my doorway." She said, leaning her head back, enjoying the feel of the hardness inside her.

The sound of her juices turned him on, the sight of her fucking herself drove him crazy but it was the sound of her voice, the nasty way she spoke to him that made him unzip his grey uniform slacks and release the beast from its resting place on his thigh.

Connors stroked his jimmy as he watched Mel beat the veggie made toy inside her. Mel loved the way the light from the moon flickered against the skin of his jimmy, the head peeking his palm. To see him, the man she'd desired so much over the last three months, stroking his jimmy up and down, with slow deliberate strokes, severely increased the height of her sexual peek.

Mel asked him to switch.

"Let me stroke that dick for you. You don't have to do that by yourself," she told him, taking the hand from his hardness and placing it on the end of the toy.

She took her hand and placed it around the bottom of his shaft and began to stroke his solidness, maneuvering her wrists at different

74

angles to stimulate him. Connors moaned at the feel of her soft palm against his flesh mixed with the sight of the toy he was now controlling; pushing it up against the rim of her cervix.

Together they watched one another, alternating between stares into one another's eyes and the pleasure growing in the palms of their hands. Connors felt himself about to explode and Mel got so excited as the veins in his jimmy began to budge against her fingers.

"That time huh? Shoot that shit baby, shoot it... shoot it all over me," she told him, taking her hand and concentrating on the rim around the head of his jimmy.

Connors stared Mel in the eyes as he squirted his juices across her stomach, trickles reaching up to her breasts. Mel rubbed it into her skin as she stared back at him, reaching her peak as well.

When it was over, he looked at Mel, the glow on her face was angelic to him. He knew at that moment that this wouldn't be the last time they encountered one another. They had already crossed so many lines, rules already broken. Yet as he rubbed his hand on her cheek and she turned to place a kiss on his palm, he told himself that he would have to see her again, soon.

Mel smiled at him as she climbed down off the washer and stood in front of him. No words were spoken between the two of them, she had nothing to say. Mel knew that he would be back; the electricity in what they had just shared assured her of that.

She closed her robe, placed her two middle fingers to her lips, kiss them and then placed them to his.

"Until next time," she said walking over to the door and removing the ladder.

She open up the door, looked out into the hallway to check and make sure the coast was clear. She looked back at Connors one last time, winked at him and headed around the corner. Connors stood there for a moment, making sure his clothes were straightened. He shook his head at the thought of what has just transpired. The creature had definitely put something on his mind... something that would change his life forever.

Charlene and Nikki walked out on the compound underneath the pavilion to release some stress via smoke. When they arrived at the row of wooden picnic tables, Tae was sitting with her headphones on, still waiting on her package to be delivered.

"You wanna hit this?" Nikki asked her, pulling her headphones off her ears and showing her the skinny white joint in her hand.

"Shitttt.... Depends, you talking 'bout hittin' that dope or hittin' that pussy?" Tae joked, handing Nikki a light.

"I keep tellin' you bitch, you ain't ready for the nutrients or the vitamins this muthafucka gush out," Nikki told her, inhaling the herbal smoke.

"You betta watch yo' mouth, you know that hoe Bright Eyes got ears like a muthafuckin' hawk."

They all look around and started laughing.

"She could be upstairs in the 2nd floor shower and hear yo' ass all t he way out here," Nikki continued teasing Tae. "You turned that bitch out in the worst way niggah. She be straight flippin' out over yo' ass. Ain't no way you would have me stuck on stupid and you ain't got at least 8 inches hangin' between yo' legs? Bitch please!"

"Damn baby, ain't nothin' wrong with being Bi, you know you wanna give it a try, I promise I won't make you cry, strap it on and it's do or die, and it ain't like you got a guy, so stop tryin' to be so fly and don't say goodbye, just let me play 'tween them thighs."

Charlene busted out laughing and hi-fived Tae.

"I heard that shit," she told Tae.

77

Nikki just chuckled and flicked both Tae and Charlene the finger.

"You hoe's insane." she said, looking around behind her to make sure the perimeter truck wasn't nearing before handing the joint to Charlene.

"What you doing out here anyway? Escaping *hurricane Bright Eyes?*" Nikki asked her.

"Naw lil' momma, it's that time. Waitin' on them headlights to roll through."

"That's what's up, you gettin' in anything good?"

Tae looked to Nikki then nodded down to her lap and back to her.

"You wanna find out what I got good? Quit beatin' around the bush. When you gone let me prop that ass up on one of them washers and hit spin cycle around that clit?"

Charlene walked off leaving them to their flirting. She knew that it would only be a matter of time before Tae talked Nikki into giving in. Charlene didn't care, she had come to love them both like family and all she wanted was for them both to be happy, no matter who it was with.

She decided that it was time she wrote Marco a letter. Between the unanswered calls and the short time allotted to talk whenever she did speak to him, sometimes writing out your feeling was the best way to handle things.

She grabbed her yellow note pad from the top shelf in her locker, grabbed a pen, plopped down on her bunk, placed her head phones over her ears and began to tell Marco how she felt.

Hey you,

I felt that maybe this was the best way to get my feelings across to you, uninterrupted and in their entirety. I love you baby, let me start off by sayin' that. More than you will ever know and I truly appreciate all you do, not only for me but our children. I want you to know that whatever you have to do to make it happen, I respect it and accept it.

It was so selfish of me to ever doubt your sincerity or love; it's just that the thought of someone else touching you kills me. Someone other than me, bouncing up and down on the dick that has belong to me since you first took my virginity. You broke this pussy in as a girl but made me yo' woman and I cannot imagine being anything other than that to you. Can't imagine someone else feelin' the pleasure you've made me feel over the years.

I've never known the touch of another man and I never want to. This pussy has always belonged to you and it always will! It's throbbing right now as I write. I've got one hand inside me and the other writing you. It's juices running across my fingers.

I miss you baby and I can't wait to feel you again.

Charlene thought back to Nikki's words, "Use that road."

Did you know it's possible to make love to me, even while I'm here? To touch me and feel me as soon as you can get here? If you drive up here and meet me at the Rec center at the bottom of the hill, we can make it happen... not only that, I can suck yo' dick again. It's been so long since I've tasted your body in my mouth and I want it baby... no, I need it.

So think about it and when I call you, let me know what you think. Don't give me a long spill about this or that... all I wanna hear you say is, yes Lena, you can have yo' dick.

Now I gotta go, I gotta make this pussy cum until you can.

Always yours,

Lena

Charlene lay back on the bed and let the sounds of Nelly fill her ears.

"... I heard a friend who a friend who told a friend of mine, that you was thinking that we should do it one mo' time. If this ain't the truth then hopefully it's not a lie cause I ain't got no issues with hittin' that another time. We never had a problem gettin' it done, disagreed upon a lot Ma but the sex wasn't one..."

Charlene folded the letter and chuckled to herself as she placed it down inside the envelope. Inmates weren't allowed to seal outgoing mail and had she been thinking clearly; not overrun by emotions, she would've realized that she had made a grave mistake. The officers on duty at the camp had the option to read all outgoing mail, so the chance of getting caught planning anything against the camp rules were severely heightened, especially when the officer on duty needed to make sure that none of your outgoing communication concerned him.

Charlene was feeling hopeful. She had done exactly what Nikki had told her, she stroked Marco's ego and if it was one thing she knew about Marco, it was that the freak in him would draw him back to her if she played her cards right.

She bounced down the back steps to the back hallway and walked past the phone room to the mailbox. As she dropped the envelope in the red wooden lockbox, she placed a kiss on the seal of the envelope. Step one of her plan to lure Marco's loyalty back to her was now complete.

As she turned to walk away from the mailbox, unbeknownst to her, the watchful eye of Tucker was upon her. She felt confident that the next time she dialed his cell there was absolutely no way Tiffany would be the voice she'd hear on the other end of the line.

Once she disappeared from his sight, Officer Tucker headed right over to the wooden box, unlocked it and retrieved the letters from inside. He went back into his office and placed the pile of envelopes on his desk. Slowly he searched through until he came across the one addressed to *Marco Cannon*.

He needed to know if Charlene had in any shape, form or fashion, mentioned the event that happened earlier. She hadn't but what she did mention was definitely enough to send her to the hole however, Tucker passed on the write up. He didn't wanna ruffle any feathers at this time. He'd let the mail slide through and if the main mail room caught it, so be it but as far as him, he decided to keep it as an ace in the hole; a little incentive to keep Charlene both in line and on her knees at his command.

Charlene looked around for Nikki outside and when she didn't see her, she assumed that she'd headed back up to the room but once she walked back inside the small 8x8 they shared, Nikki was no where to be found.

Charlene put her music on and lay back against her pillow. The days would be long until Marco received his letter and she was able to call him. As she listened to Gerald Levert playing on the local station, she began thinking of her plan to get down to the Rec center undetected and back.

"...I remember our first date, our first argument. Our very first break up to make up that got me to this moment. And every girlfriend and every one night stand, every heart ache and every heart break, led me to you, drove me to you, it made me better, better suited for you... it had to be, my destiny..."

Marco had been the only lover Charlene had ever known and she couldn't bring herself to phantom her life without him. Trying to wrap her mind around him being with someone else was hard. She always had somehow pictured this shoe on the opposite foot. That it could one day be him, locked away for the lifestyle he provided for them, her trying her best to hold out until he returned home. She never wondered would she be faithful; never doubted that she would have been there for him in spite of who she allowed between her legs in his absence. She never dreamed she'd be lying in her prison dorm, dealing with him and another woman.

She stared off at the wall trying not to cry. She knew that just as Nikki said, she had to suck up his current situation while she was locked down.

"What you thinkin' about Mommi, *yo' boo* again?"

Charlene pulled the ear phones from her head.

"Where you been? I went outside looking for you but I ain't see you."

"I was playin' look out for Tae's ass at the bottom of the hill from the perimeter truck. Dat damn girl is a hustler to the tenth power. I got somethin' hot from her too. She probably gone charge me some pussy for it but shitttt, she just might get it for this one," Nikki teased, lifting her shirt and pulling out the Samsung cellular phone from down inside her panties.

"*Bitch*, is that a phone? Do it work?" Charlene asked, jumping from her bunk, wide eyed.

"It's got a lil charge, let's see. Lay back on da bed, take them sweats off, pull yo' panties to the side and let's take a pussy shot and send it to yo' Boo's phone," Nikki told her, looking down the hallway to make sure no one was coming before she closed the door and placed the white terry cloth bathrobe over the window once again.

"Are you serious right now?"

"Fuck yeah, is it or is it not gone be the fuckin' surprise of his life? Plus he don't know this number so even if she do pick up his phone that bitch gone flip cause she damn sho' ain't gone think it's you. She gone think that niggah got some other hoe sending him pictures of her pussy, the bitch gone freak out and all hell gone break loose."

Charlene high-fived Nikki.

"Now lay back bitch and spread that pussy open."

Nikki took three photos of Charlene's mommy, one with her fingers inside the pink opening, spreading her lips apart. They added no text when they attached the images to a *multi media* message and hit *send*.

Charlene didn't know what to expect when she sent the explicit photos, knowing that the gesture could come back to bite her in the ass if he responded in any other way than she hoped he would. After all Nikki was right, Marco didn't know this number.

"You ever thought about fuckin' with a woman as long as you been locked down Nikki? I see the way you and Tae keep teasin' each other."

"And what makes you think I haven't, just because I don't walk around advertising my business like these other crazy hoes? Hell I've had women before... women, guards, visitors... all that. In the FCI I was poppin' bitch but all it brought me was a whole lot of fuckin' drama.

Hoes is crazier than niggah's. They emotional by nature anyway. Add that to the fact of all the shit they go through being locked down, away from home and shit; you got a recipe for muthafuckin' disaster. Hoes mad cause they know you fuckin' the guard and he ain't giving them the time of day so them hoes dry snitchin' and shit; mad cause they ain't getting' the dick. Locks, razors, all kinds of crazy shit; committing violations just to stay behind with another bitch cause you worried if she gone fuck yo' enemy as soon as yo' ass leave? Ain't no fuckin' way boo. They can have all that shit. This here is gone be my peace-of-mind end of my bid… and ain't none of these hoes worth that, feel me?"

Charlene shook her head as the phone vibrated inside Nikki's hand. Nikki looked down at the message.

How the fuck you pull that off in there? And who the fuck took these pics?

"Damn bitch, that niggah know his pussy," she laughed.

Charlene grabbed the phone and began answering him.

My rm mate took em 4 me. How in da fuck did u know it was me?

Stp it.. I been eatin' dat pussy ovr 14rs. I knw what it look like. Plus u da only one I knw wit a mole on ur middle finger at da base of ur nail…btw, dat pussy look so fuckin pretty.

Charlene smiled. No it wasn't the words she wanted to hear him say but it was better than nothing, And Charlene figured that if she had to use a few tricks to get him to come around so be it.

Wow, dats whats up bae. Dis my Bunkie phone so Ima shake but u keep dat n heads up, I sent u a letter dat I need to make sure U get.

Charlene handed the phone back to Nikki who was taking apart one of her shaving razors to remove the blade. She began cutting a slit into the edge of her mattress so she could stash the phone down inside.

Before she could turn it off Marco sent another text… this one of his multicolored penis, standing rock solid at attention.

84

The things u can still do 2 me. Dats the Lena I luv.

"*Damn* he gotta big dick! No wonder yo' ass in here flippin'!" Nikki joked.

Charlene grabbed the phone back from Nikki and deleted the photo but not before she spent a moment to salivate over the beauty of the organ that had brought her so much pleasure over the years.

"I told you that niggah wasn't going anywhere didn't I?"

"Yes you did... when he get that letter and meet me down at the bottom of that hill, I'ma make sure of that!"

Tae walked down the 2East hallway and as she passed the dorm room, Bright Eyes peeked her head out of the eight man dorm room she had been assigned to by Ms. Garrett.

"Hey you, what's your room number?"

Tae stopped, turned back and entered Bright Eyes room.

"206, down the hall."

"Well when you're settled, I'm ready for that shower if you are."

Tae thought back to what Ms. Crumple said, *it comes with bullshit and drama* and began to second guess the flirtatious ride she'd boarded with Bright Eyes. Kelly had asked her to stay true; not to hurt her because she'd wait as long as she had too so long as Tae remained true.

"About that shower, as tempting as that sounds lil momma…"

Her words were halted as Bright Eyes began to strip right in front of her in the dorm room. She slid off her pants and once Tae saw her unleash the beast of booty she had inside those powder blue scrubs, all sense of reasoning went out the window.

"Damn sexy, uh on second thought, gimme about ten minutes and I'm on the way," she said, shaking her head at the sight before her. "*Damn!*"

Tae walked down to her room and looked around. She could tell that whoever was her new roommate was, she was a neat freak. The floors were waxed so good you could see your reflection on them. Handmade burgundy and white curtains were up to the small metal framed window with a matching crocheted blanket; the University of Alabama's logo stitched inside and two matching throw pillows on the bottom bunk. Her roommate had taken the liberty of making Tae's bunk for her and had placed a crocheted burgundy rose on her pillow.

Tae looked on the locker in front of her and picked up the burgundy and white picture frame made from plastic canvas. Inside was a picture of a nice looking older woman holding a young boy on her lap.

As Tae set the frame down, in walked a young fair skinned woman with a wavy low cut fade; tatted more than most and sporting crushed diamonds in her front teeth. As soon as the Mexican inmate introduced herself Tae knew they had one true thing in common, women.

"What's up bruh, I'm Meko, you?"

"Tae."

"Cool, well welcome to the penthouse homey, been a minute since I've had a roomy. Honey's been trying like a muthafucka though you know what I'm sayin'? But Ms. C' knew I ain't want the headache. Whose yo'
counselor?"

"Ms. C," they laughed.

"That's what's up. I guess she figured since we both deal with women, we'd be a good fit."

"No doubt," Tae said, throwing her things on the top bunk.

"My lady comes by and clean the room everyday so you ain't gotta worry about that. She cooks and do laundry too so whatever you need, just let me know, I got you."

Tae gave Meko some dap.

"Roll Tide huh?" Tae asked her, nodding towards her blanket.

"No other way bruh," Meko said, popping the shoulder blades of her freshly creased light grey t-shirt. "You ball?"

"Do a cow piss milk?"

They burst out laughing as Shawna tapped on the door with a mound of toiletries in her hand. Body wash, toothpaste, lotion, hair grease, a tooth brush, shower shoes, shower cap, razors, shampoo, conditioner, comb, brush, a new pair of ankle socks, a beach towel and hair gel. She handed a shower caddy to Tae and then laid all the items from her arms on the top of Tae's locker.

"This should be a good start," she told Tae, handing her a glass vile of fragrance oil. "I don't know how you like to smell but I'd sure love to smell it on you."

"And the parade begins," Meko smirked.

Shawna flicked Meko the finger. Tae smiled and looked at the vile in Shawna's hand, *CK1* by Calvin Kline.

"Dig that," she said, looking to Meko who was standing behind Shawna's back rubbing her fingers together, insinuating that Shawna had money and liked to spend it.

Before Tae could respond, Bright Eyes stepped in the doorway wearing nothing but a towel around her. She looked at Shawna, and then to Tae, who looked from Shawna to Meko to Bright Eyes.

"Damn," Mcko whispered.

Bright Eyes was a very attractive woman, as was Shawna but then Shawna wasn't standing in front of her wearing nothing but her birthday suit.

"This you bruh?" Meko asked.

Tae looked at Bright Eyes and then to Meko.

"She a free agent for now but I'm thinking about signing her to my roster."

"Word up bruh, don't leave all that out there on the market too long cause I'm sayin' tho... good Lawd!"

Bright Eyes walked into the room over Tae's locker, grabbed the toiletries and filled the caddy Tae was holding in her hand much to the distaste of Shawna. She looked at Tae, took the caddy from her hand and smiled.

"I'm ready to shower," she told her, walking past Shawna and smirking.

"Thanks love," she told her, lifting the caddy up towards her.

"Dammmnnnn," Meko laughed. "She somethin' else ain't she?" she joked putting her hand over her mouth. "I see this gone be an interesting living arrangement."

Tae looked to Meko and shook her head.

"Don't sweat the small. I promised her I'd share some lather with her. Can't have my friend shit around here living foul, feel me? Thanks again though baby, I got somethin' special on the horizon for you, no doubt."

Tae grabbed the beach towel, the shower shoes and headed out the room. Shawna looked to Meko who just shrugged her shoulders.

"Not an issue, I'll get it."

Meko snickered.

"Shit u better show up lookin' better than that bitch that just left here when you come for it, that's for damn sho'!" she teased.

Bright Eyes was in the shower lathering her body when Tae slid the curtain to the side. She just stood there for a moment, looking at the exotic creature before her.

"Damn yo' sexy ass make that lather look good," she said watching the white foam slide down her body.

"I thought we were sharing," Bright Eyes told her, pulling her inside.

Shawna's first thought was too dry snitch to get Bright Eyes in trouble but the only problem with that was, Tae would get in trouble as well and that's not what she wanted. She wanted to befriend Tae and hopefully one day become more than friends.

She had been going through so much since her last companion had left the compound. Her three children had been taken from the aunt she'd left them with and placed in the custody of the State of Indiana. Since Shawna was a lifer, she and her husband had lost all parental rights to the children because DFS didn't hold cases open past two years.

Shawna and her husband had ran a meth lab and had been labeled *Kingpins* by the Federal guidelines and thus handed down the mandatory life sentences but since the crime was non-violent, Shawna was allowed to be housed at the camp with her husband at the neighboring FMC.

To keep the children from going to a foster home and possibly being separated, Shawna and her husband had left the children in the custody of her aunt. For the last two years however DFS had been heavily involved in her children's lives due to reports of drug use by her aunt and sexual abuse reported by her eldest daughter, nine year old Krystal.

Shawna did her best to keep it together in front of her peers but at night she cried all the time. Because she'd been in the camp for a few years, she'd worked her way up to one of the camps few single bed rooms; which was good because it kept people out of her business.

None more so than the addiction she developed to Oxycodone pills after her children were taken away. Once they were taken, she had no idea where they were nor with whom they were with… and not to know where your children are, whose watching them, is anyone harming them, not being able to talk to them on birthdays, Christmas and Mother's Day was heart wrenching. The only thing that could make that worse was to have a roommate that could. Countless stories of wonderful visits, photos plastered everywhere and how little Johnny took his first steps was just too much for Shawna to handle.

To cope she started abusing the Oxycodone pills that she gotten slipped in through visits with her brother. For the most part she kept it under wraps and with documented medical records of migraines, she was able to get refills of Ibuprofen 800's which were the same color, shape and size as her illegal medicine so hiding them was never a problem. Shawna also sold them to other inmates, which was how she kept her books stacked and able to give Tae anything she wanted or needed within the camp's capacity.

For now, she'd allow Bright Eyes to think she was winning the game when in reality; she was only ahead in the inning. Shawna knew women like Tae, therefore she knew that they required the finer things, regardless of their environment and clearly it was Shawna, not Bright Eyes that could provide that for her, at least that's what Shawna thought.

Tae and Bright Eyes showered, washed one another, kissed one another, and teased one another. Tae pressed Bright Eyes up against the shower wall underneath the shower head, allowing the hot water to roll down her breasts into the palm of her hand folded into a canal leading into Bright Eyes' mommy.

Tae had her fingers inside her cave. Bright Eyes squirmed and grinded her hips against the feel of Tae's soft fingers plunging inside her. Tae whispered in her ear.

"I told you I was gonna clean it out for you."

"Yes... yes you did Boo," Bright Eyes panted.

Tae pulled back to kiss her.

"This what you wanted huh? Is this why you came to my room wit' yo' pussy hanging out?"

Through moans of mounting pleasure, Bright Eyes answered, "I want whatever you got for me."

Tae kneeled down and lifted one of Bright Eyes legs over her left shoulder and with her right hand; she spread her lips apart to do a quick inspection of her mommy. She checked for bumps, blisters, old scarring and any discoloration of the skin. She stuck her tongue out and began to flick it soft but quickly against her clit; the hot water streaming down against her face.

Tae liked the idea of sucking pussy underneath the waterfall. She took her left hand and slid around to Bright Eyes' ass and then returned her right fingers up inside her.

92

Slowly but forcefully she finger fucked her while messaging her clit with her tongue. Bright Eyes gripped her head with a death grip as Tae felt her clit began to swell in her mouth. Faster and faster Bright Eyes rocked her hips until she felt her pressure about to escape. She dug her nails into Tae's shoulders, panting uncontrollably and trying to catch the breath caught in her chest. The energy seemed to drain from inside her as her knees threatened to give way from underneath her.

Tae stood up, kissed her passionately and forcefully. Bright Eyes looked into Tae's eyes and for a moment the look on her face was reminiscent of Kelly's look the first time she'd made love to her. She leaned back.

"Yo' first?"

"My first and it felt so fuckin' good."

A "turnout" could be a blessing or a curse... and Tae was about to find out which one. When they exited the shower and walked into the hallway, Tae gave Bright Eyes a peck on the cheek. She told Tae that once she dressed she'd be down to her room. Tae however was ready to hit the compound and see what was going on.

"I'm a go see what's poppin' out on the grounds and we'll hook up later," Tae told a disappointed Bright Eyes.

Shawna came up the back stairwell just as Tae reached her room.

"You blow smoke?"

"Shit, do a chimney in the winter," Tae joked.

"Get dressed and come on outside. I got somethin' for you."

"Come on in," Tae told her.

Bright Eyes called after Tae and headed down the hall, huffing and puffing all the way. Tae backed up out the room and raised her eyebrow to a ranting Bright Eyes.

"What is that about?" she said, pointing to Shawna.

"Hold up, what you on? We about to go blow some herbs. You wanna come?"

"I don't have enough," Shawna spit out as Bright Eyes rolled her eyes.

Tae turned to Shawna and told her to give her a minute. That she'd be down as soon as she got her clothes on.

"You know that hoe like you, why you even entertaining her? I thought me and you was on somethin'."

Tae took a step back, bewildered by her comment.

"Are you really serious right now? You wanted to link up, I wanted to link up, we did that. No money down."

"No money down, what the fuck that mean?"

"It means no strings attached lil momma. Now yeah I'm feelin' you, tried and true but you can't come at me like that, all aggressive and shit. We gel, aight? But the only one I owe any loyalty too is back at home, so don't make that mistake, aight? I'm gone have friends and hang out so if you can't handle that I suggest you rethink signing with this squad."

Bright Eyes looked at Tae confusingly.

How can she act like that after what just happened? Didn't it mean anything to her?

"You right, I don't have a hold on you but I thought what we just shared was something other than a random hit. I'm sayin' I know you don't get down like this with er'body right?"

"You more than right lil' momma, you tru on that one. Which is why I'm trying to figure out why you standing' here trippin'. It's a smoke, now chill out and I'll fuck with you later. Damn, these lips keep me in shit," she joked, trying to make Bright Eyes smile. "And I ain't even blessed you with the best yet."

"That shit ain't funny to me," she said, turning and walking out the room. "Can you not be long so we can fill out these slips?"

Tae shook her head.

"This one might be a problem," she joked to herself.

Tae stood back and scratched her head. Would that ten minutes of pleasure come back to haunt her in the worst way… one thing was for sure, she would soon find out.

With four am count time ending, Mel climbed down from her bunk, put on her house shoes and quietly walked down the hallway to the officer's station. It was Officer Connor's second rotation at the camp and the way things were left between them, Mel knew that it was time to take control of what she wanted. All the flirtations, the illegal touching in passing, the smiles, the inside jokes but more so the feel of his skin in her hands… it was time to cash in.

She was dressed in a pair of shorts made from cut off sweats with her cheeks hanging out the bottom and a cut off wife beater made into a halter top, no panties, and no bra; her nipples peeking through the thin white material. When she rounded the doorway Connors smiled at the sight before him.

"Come in," he told Mel pushing his papers to the side of his desk.

Mel stepped inside and sat down in one of the square grey metal framed chairs facing him. Officer Connors straightened the scarlet red tie on his neck.

"How you been? Haven't seen you in six months?"

"Yeah, I tried to get back sooner, trust me but you know how that seniority shit works. "

"And why it is you were trying to get back sooner?"

Officer Connors dropped his head and chuckled.

"I needed to check and see if the uhhh, washers were working in the laundry room. I was concerned about you washing yo' clothes," he laughed.

"Ohhh and I just bought some detergent too. I'd be more than happy to help you with that. Actually I was about to put a load in, seeing as though I ran out of panties to put on," Mel said, pulling the loose shorts to the side, exposing a cleanly shaven smooth vagina.

The lights in the office were off so Connors took his flashlight from his waist and aimed it between Mel's legs. She lifted her right leg up onto the arm of the chair next to her to give him a full view of her mommy. Connors' jimmy grew instantly inside his heather grey uniform slacks.

This time he wasn't watching her from a distance as she lay in her bed nor in the laundry room as she sat on top of the washer. No, this time he was up close and personal. He could hear the sounds of her wetness as she played inside her walls with her fingers.

"Spread your lips apart," he told her, reaching down and increasing the volume of the mini boom box he brought to work with him.

He rubbed his hand across his hardness as Mel spread her lips apart and pulled them backwards to pop her clit from its hiding place. The juices on her fingers were glistening against the light from the flashlight. The local station was playing LSG's *My Body* as Connors went over to the doorway, looked out into the hallway to make sure no one was coming and then closed the door once he saw that the coast was clear.

He walked back over to the chair and stood behind Mel, the smell of his Ralph Lauren cologne was so intoxicated to her. He slid his hands down the sides of her arms and pulled them back up, running his fingers around her cheeks to her mouth. Mel wrapped her tongue around his finger before inserting it into her mouth. She felt his solidness pressing up against the nape of her neck and it turned her on, tremendously. He ran his free hand down the front of her halter top and squeezed her bra-less breasts. Pinching her nipple in between his fingers. Mel's mommy was contracting as he moaned and pushed his jimmy against her.

The feel of her nipples, the wetness of her mouth along with the sight of her finger fucking herself was driving him crazy.

"... how would you like it if I laid you down, would you like if I was to sex you down? I can't think about nothin' else you saturate me with yo' love..."

Mel wanted more from him. She had waited six months for this moment to present itself again and she planned to take full advantage of it. She wanted to feel him inside her. She pulled his finger from her mouth.

"Let me be everything you ain't got at home. Let me be the freak I know she's not. Do to me what she won't let you do to her." Mel told him, moving the chair to the side and now standing in front of him, his hands now in her shorts.

"Feel me, feel how wet you make this pussy. If you gonna risk it, risk it all! Get yo' money's worth baby. Feel me, any and everywhere you want too... my pussy, my mouth, my ass... what you want, huh," she asked him, nibbling on his neck. "What you need daddy?"

Connors melted at the sound of her voice in his ear. No he didn't get the freak he desired at home. His wife was raised in the Old Testament of the Bible in church. Missionary was the only position she believed in and oral sex was definitely out of the question.

She was pure when he'd met her however and she was now carrying his child. He loved the fact that she was one of the few wholesome women left and he took pride in knowing he was the only one who had been in between her legs but there was a need she couldn't fulfill, the need to be as nasty as he wanted to be. After all he was a man, with fantasies and desires he knew he'd

98

never be able to fulfill with her. So here he was standing in front of a woman with the eagerness and desire to please him, the body of a video vixen and an invitation for him to enter it in every way imaginable.

Mel stroked the nine inches of raw flesh in her hand, feeling the ribbing of the shaft against her hand's movement. Connor threw his head back and enjoyed the familiar feel of her fingers.

"I've been a naughty girl Officer Connors. I've broken the rules," she said, speeding up the rhythm of her hand, twisting her wrist; his body pumping in response. "Don't you wanna arrest me, discipline me… come on, cuff me. I deserve it, I fucked up."

Connors reached behind his back and grabbed the cuffs from their holsters in his waist belt and with his jimmy still inside her hand, slapped the cuffs on her wrists.

"Naughty huh? How naughty?"

"As naughty as you want me to be," she said, stroking her fingers in a circle and gliding them against the rim of his jimmy.

He moaned out.

"Shit, you under arrest."

"For what?"

"For being the baddest bitch on this compound. You been charged," he said spinning her around to face the desk. "Tried," he told her, snatching her shorts to the side and slamming her upper body down onto the desk.

"Convicted," he said, forcing his jimmy inside the tight walls of her mommy. "Sentenced, to be my bitch," he commanded, grabbing her around the waist and slamming against her ass; Mel's wetness gushing from inside her.

It was exciting to her, to feel him thrusting inside her, her wrists cuffed as she pushed her ass back into him. She felt him deep within her walls. He wrapped his hand over her mouth to muffle her sound as he snatched her up to him, bent his knees and drove his jimmy deep inside her. He wrapped his other hand around her throat and choked her.

"... wanna fill you up till yo' river flows all over me, wanna feel your precious treasure wrapped around me oh so tightly...in...out... wanna hear you shout... so come on baby let me break you off...guaranteed I'll turn you out...."

"You wanna be my fantasy huh? You wanna gimme this pussy and that mouth huh? What you want me to do in that mouth huh? You want me to shoot this nut down that throat, huh?"

Connors pulled from inside her, feeling himself about to explode. He spun her around and told her to lie back on the desk. He lifted her legs upon his shoulders and re-entered her wetness. He wrapped his hands around her thighs and pulverized her. Everything he had thought about the past six months, all the want, all the desire, all the wishful thinking, everything he longed to do to his wife but was forbidden, he took out on the beautiful young creature in front of him.

He spread her legs further apart and felt himself threaten to erupt once again. He didn't want to take that chance so Connors pulled her up to him and swallowed her mouth inside his own; his braces clattering up against her teeth.

Mel whispered in his ear.

"I'm about to cum, don't stop, please... don't stop baby... it's been so long... please let me cum on this dick… please."

100

Mel pushed him from inside her and told him to let her legs down. She stood up and told him to sit down against the edge of the desk. Mel pulled the chair over in front of her and leaned over onto the arms of the chair.

"Put that dick back in," she instructed him as she lifted her legs onto the outside of his, wrapped her ankles around his calves and used her leg muscles to bounce up and down on his jimmy. As she began to cum down his jimmy, she gripped him tighter inside her legs.

Up and down she went, twisting and twirling her hips until she felt him once again about to burst. She moaned out in pleasure as his jimmy hit her cervix and sent shock waves throughout her body. Connor was in awe of how Mel worked her body. He watched her ass move, her hips sway and he couldn't retrain himself any further, he couldn't tell her to stop.

When her moans grew in volume he again grabbed her around her mouth and told her to quiet down.

"Shut the fuck up. Bite down on my finger, bite it."

Mel bit down on his finger like a man being circumcised with no anesthetic and a stick in his mouth. The pressure sent a surge of pain down his body and Connors loved the intensity. He lifted off the desk, grabbed Mel around her waist with one arm, her upper body with the other and pounded her, mid-air until he could hold it no more. He bit down on the bottom of her neck and damn near drew blood as he began pumping months of dreams, thoughts and fantasies of this moment, inside her.

He bit down harder as he exploded in her mommy. Mel squeezed the chair with all her might, trying not to scream. It had been a long time since she'd had a dick inside her and even longer since she had one that she desired and wanted. He had turned out to be better than her imagination hoped he would be and she let him know it; her juices and muffled sounds mixing with his.

When he released her down to her feet, Mel felt their juices run down the inside of her legs. She looked at the front of his pants and nodded towards the mess they had made.

"You might wanna take care of that," she chuckled to him, trying to catch her breath as he un-cuffed her wrists.

The back of her neck was throbbing from his braces and Mel told him she had to go tend to waterfall between her legs. She told him she would bring him a hot towel back. She walked over to the door, cracked it and once she saw the coast was clear she hurried down to her room around the corner, grabbed a wash rag from the rail of her bunk, body wash and her square magnetic mirror from her locker.

She walked into the bathroom over to the sink and turned on the faucet and pulled her hair up into a ponytail. Mel turned her back to the mirror over the sink, held up her hand mirror and looked at the back of her neck. The wound was red with clear marks of his braces and scrapes to her skin. Mel just smiled at the sight. The burning of the scraped skin turned her on tremendously, she didn't know why but it excited her.

She took the wet rag, wrung it out and placed it against her neck. She almost had another orgasm as the pain surged through her senses; inviting them to engage in this mesmerizing feeling over and over again.

She washed the blood specks from the rag and added some body wash to the cotton cloth, preparing to take it to him so he could clean up and she could get back to her room.

"Damn baby, I didn't mean to get you like that," Connors said softly, standing in the doorway.

He had his navy blue sweater tied around his waist hiding the wet spot on the front of his pants as best he could.

"No worries," she whispered back. "It'll heal up."

Connors nodded his head towards the bathroom stall. Seeing the trauma he caused to her skin made his jimmy hard once again. He looked both ways down the hall before he entered the grey and white painted, six stall bath room. He told Mel to go turn on the shower furthest from the door while he waited in the stall closest to the wall. Mel took off her shorts and wife beater and threw them onto the floor by the shower stall and hurried her naked body over to an awaiting Connors in the stall.

Inside the stall he removed his sweater, wrapped his keys up inside it and placed them on the back of the toilet. He looked at her neck again and stretched out his tongue and licked the blood from the wound. At that moment they found out they shared the pleasure of pain as he slammed

Mel against the door grey metal, kissed her mouth with an intensity that almost took her breath away. She pushed him down onto the stall, removed his jimmy from his pants, lifted her frame on top of him and worked his jimmy back inside her as he leaned back to plant his black work shoes on the stall door.

Mel wrapped her arms around his neck and began to ride him as he wet his finger and played with the opening of her ass. They froze as they heard another stall door close. Mel put her fingers to her lips and took over the moment with slow, deliberate strokes; the heels of her feet on the toilet seat behind him and her hands on his knees.

She rocked and rocked against his body as they looked into one another's' eyes; finding themselves in forbidden waters with circling sharks that neither cared about. When they heard the toilet flush, Mel sat still for a moment before climbing down from his hardness and turning around to face the door.

She bent downward and watched as the white terry cloth house shoes walked out the rest room. She kept her hands on the floor and once again instructed him to return his jimmy inside her walls. She began controlled movement as he returned his finger to her ass. The pleasure of pain returned to her as she squirmed about, feeling the pressure build inside her.

The atmosphere, the smell of their essence blending together along with the inability to allow sound to come from their mouths set them on fire for one another and when they exploded this time Mel jumped up from his jimmy, spun around and took him deep within her jaws as Connors dug his nails inside her back.

She arched her back in pain as she swallowed his seed, effortless and gag-less. Connors was in a trance as Mel looked up at him, licked her lips and smiled.

"Anything you want, anything you need, it's yours, you hear me? It's yours. You gone be mines, you hear me?" he asked her kissing her on her lips, loving the taste of their sex she wore as lip gloss.

"I already am. I was yours the moment I laid eyes on you."

They had to part ways. It was coming up on 5:15 am and soon the inmates that worked in the kitchen would be up and getting ready for work, including herself.

"I'm off tonight but then on the next three. I'll see you then," he told her, kissing her again before he straightened himself and left out the stall.

Mel waited a few minutes then went over to the shower. She placed her hand down between her thighs and felt the stickiness of their juices on her flesh. She thought about stepping in but decided against it. She didn't want to wash his smell, his saliva nor nut from her body. She wanted it to last as long as it could. She put on her clothes, crept back to her room, climbed up to her bunk, put her hand to her chest and inhaled his scent from her shirt. She couldn't believe what had just transpired between them.

In her line of work at home, rarely did she get the opportunity to sleep with someone that she desired, approached or was even attracted too. It was mostly business and the fact that she went after him and got him, in ways she never thought she could, made what had just happened all the more better. Mel felt on top of the world…. but soon, like any other thing in life that seemed too good to be true, it would all threaten to come crashing down.

Chapter Thirteen

Her stomach had been fluttering all day in anticipation of Marco's arrival. When he'd texted Nikki's phone after receiving her letter, he'd responded to Charlene's enjoyment in the exact way she requested.

Yes, you can have yo' dick... I'll be there sat.

Nikki laughed as she read the message.

"What I tell you bitch, don't no niggah want they pussy runnin' rampant. And even though you in here, now he knows you can fuck if you really wanted to. He knew better than to turn that down," she chuckled.

Charlene had spent the day pampering herself. She went to the camp's beauty shop and got her hair permed and flat ironed, and then went to her friend Jackie's room to get a manicure and pedicure. People often think that women on the inside looked like the images that TV showed of prison... rough, hair nappy, crusty and not lady like but it was quite the opposite. You could find some of the most resourceful women in the world.

Where there was access to office supplies, crafts and food, anything was could happen... lipstick and hair dye from *Kool Aid*, nail designs from *White Out*, Christmas decorations such as tinsel and water paint colors along with clothing made from old sheets and yarn including very sexy lingerie outfits.

Charlene was getting white tips on her nails and toes. Jackie would take a thin brush she'd trimmed off an old polish brush and create any professional design look you saw in a magazine. From the outside you'd think Charlene had just left the Chinese shop.

After her nails and feet dried, Charlene grabbed her razor and showered. She shaved her legs, under her arms and then her mommy. She wanted to be as smooth as a baby's bottom when Marco touched her. After she shaved, she took the opportunity to relieve some pressure. It was a known fact that the hot pulsating water of the prison shower beating down on your clit brought quick and intense orgasms.

Charlene wanted to release the initial one so that she would be more sexually relaxed when Marco put in work. She wanted him to work for it. As the water beat against the sensitive mound of flesh, mental thoughts of him danced in her head. How he used to grip her underneath her pelvis as he thrust deep inside her. How he bent her forward and made her grip his ankles between her legs for full access.

Charlene's felt her legs quiver and she fought to silence the scream building inside her. As relief pulsated from her body, she felt as if she was floating above her body.

After she returned to her room, she oiled her body down with baby oil then Tommy Girl fragrance oil, put on her light grey creased t-shirt and her dark grey shorts that stopped right below her ass cheeks. She wanted to be certain that if all they had time to do was pull her shorts to the side and fuck, Marco would have a free entry.

Nikki and Tae would be her lookouts. Nikki would watch for the perimeter truck and if any other cars came down the road, she would signal Tae, who would be hiding by the front door. Tae in turn would launch rocks at the center's front door or the window next to it to alert Charlene of incoming traffic.

Inside the Rec center were rows of round tables used for events and meetings, a full kitchen equipped with long marble topped counters and a fully equipped weight room. For this to go off without a hitch, it had to be close to ten pm count when the perimeter guard was heading to the main men's institution for count. That left a thirty minute window tops.

107

Charlene and Marco would have to either utilize the meeting area or the kitchen so that they were able to hear the rock hit the door or glass. The weight room had a door of its own for entrance so it was understandably off limits. If an officer or a family member pulled up, Tae would launch the rocks at the door but Charlene wouldn't be able to come out, she'd have to hide and take the chance of not getting caught. Marco however was dressed in workout attire and Charlene had already given him the name of an officer that he could use as his relative in case anyone asked.

As Tae and Nikki separated at the bottom of the hill, Tae smiled and smacked Nikki on the ass.

"This could be us but you be stunting' and shit," she laughed.

"Just get yo ass over there and watch my home girl's back. What you mad cause somebody finna get some real dick around this muthafucka?"

"I don't need a real one to make you scream like I got one."

Nikki waved her off as she crossed the concrete road and stood behind the trunk of a huge Oak tree to watch for approaching cars, especially the perimeter truck.

Marco had been waiting in his black Chevy Tahoe for almost an hour. When he saw Charlene run across the parking lot, he exited his truck as Tae waved him over.

"Gone get that pussy homey but nut quick. You ain't got no time to be slow dickin' and shit. You got to *Nutri Bullet* that pussy, hard and fast cause if a rock hit that door, you got seconds to zip and whip feel me?"

Marco gave Tae some dap and laughed as he entered the Rec center door.

Charlene was sitting on the edge of the kitchen counter top, leaning back on her elbows, legs spread apart and heels resting on the counter top. Marco rubbed his growing hardness as he walked towards her. He untied the string in the waistband of his navy blue Polo sweats and released jimmy, letting it bounce at attention as he reached her.

Marco leaned between Charlene's legs and snatched a fist full of her hair, pulling her up to him. No time for talking as he devoured her with his tongue aggressively. As he tongue fucked her, he slid his hand between her thighs to find her mommy, cleanly shaven and unguarded. He pushed his fingers inside, flicking the two back and forth against her walls as he continued to pulverize her with his tongue.

Charlene gripped him around the back of his neck and rocked her pelvis against his fingers. It felt so damn good to her. She grabbed the white Polo t-shirt he was wearing and almost ripped it from his body.

Everything she'd felt since finding out about Tiffany, came forth in every grip... anger, hurt, betrayal, disloyalty, want and need.... love. Charlene loved him and she let him know it as she whispered in his ear.

"I been thinkin' about you all day. I couldn't wait to touch you and feel you; to put yo' dick in my mouth and taste yo' nut running down the back of my throat."

Marco moaned as he released her and pushed her back onto the counter.

"Not yet, not till' I taste this pussy."

Knowing time was restricted, Marco rushed his lips to Charlene's throbbing clit with a force that took her breath away. She gripped the back of his head; the sneaking, the anticipation of hearing a rock tap the window, the threat of getting caught; the rush was an unbelievable feeling. Marco widened his mouth and sucked her lips inside his along with her clit and used his rolling tongue to massage her clit until she could hold it no more.

She couldn't scream, so she tightened her legs around his head, dug her nails into his back and Marco raised her ass off the counter as he stood up, gripping her legs around his shoulders. Suspended in air, Charlene could stay silent no more.

She screamed so loud Tae could hear her on the other side of the door. Tae snickered to herself, knowing how much this visit meant to her friend. She would have to experience this pleasure with Kelly someday soon she told herself, if they pulled this off.

Inside Marco pulled Charlene to him, leaving her legs around his shoulders. He reached down and pushed his jimmy inside her and Charlene almost lost it. It had been years since she felt his hardness slam against her cervix and it felt like heaven to her. Marco gripped her around the waist, spent around and slammed her back against the beige colored drywall behind him. He dove into the warmth of her walls.

"Shit Lena, this pussy so fuckin' good. It feels so hot in this muthafucka. You miss this dick? Tell me you miss this dick," he commanded as he put a slight bend in his knees to allow her legs to fall from his shoulders into the cradle of his arms.

He took a step backwards to allow her shoulders to slide down the wall but remain against it. Charlene panted as Marco slammed all nine inches of rock hard dick inside her; banging against her body in frustration... frustration for her being away... for him having to miss her.

"You know I miss this dick baby. It's the only dick I know. This big muthafucka is fucking the shit outta me. This yo' pussy, you know that don't you? Ummm... tell me... tell me... tell me you know this is yo' pussy baby."

Marco let her down from his arms and gripped her by the back of her head and walked her over to the round tables in the meeting rooms. He slammed her chest first on to the chilled table, yanked her shorts to the side once more and shoved his jimmy back inside her. The table produced Charlene's ass at the perfect angle of entry where Marco could feel all of her walls, the tip of his jimmy poking the bottom of her mommy.

"This gon' always be my pussy no matter what. It's always been," he said grabbing the back of her shirt and pulling her towards him. "Always will be; I make this pussy flow," he told her forcing her down to his favorite position.

She reached between her legs and gripped his ankles and Marco for the moment, was home. He took in every inch of her. Her juices swishing against the hardness of his jimmy insanely turned him on. He was nearing his mark and Charlene could feel him swell inside her. She yanked away from him, spun around, slid a chair over, sat down and in one swoop had his jimmy to the back of his throat. Just like riding a bike, Charlene picked up right where she'd left off with him. She knew exactly how to make his knees buckle. How could she not? He was the one who taught her exactly how to pleasure him orally.

Charlene took his hands, placed them around her head and gripped the back of his thighs, guiding him in and out of her throat, relaxing her tonsils so he could slide the tip of his jimmy down her esophagus with ease. She allowed the spit from her mouth to fall from her jaws to the floor below. She felt him about to explode.

Marco put a death grip on her neck and violently thrust his jimmy inside her mouth until he felt the nut shoot from deep inside his balls, down his jimmy and into her throat.

111

"Ohhhhhh baby fuuuccccckkkk... oh you makin' this dick buss....
ohhhh I'm cumin' babyyyyy... get it... get it all... swallow that
nut," he told her, as she used a swallowing motion to pull the nut
from his jimmy.

Marco's knees were getting weaker and weaker with every motion
she made with her throat muscles. Charlene made sure she'd gotten
every drop and she kept sucking until he forced her to release it
with a push to her shoulder.

Time was almost up and Charlene had only minutes to say what
she wanted to say but she chose to remain silent and allowed what
they had just experienced together speak on its own. She stood up,
fixed her shorts and walked up to a panting Marco. She kissed him
on the lips and told him she had to go.

"You're safe to leave, just give me about a six minute head start
ok? Love you," she told him, kissing her two fingers and placing
them against his lips.

When she got to the door, she looked back at him one final time,
told him she loved him once more and left out. She ducked behind
the metal barrel with Tae and when Tae lit up her cell phone and
flashed it at Nikki, Nikki looked around the area and then told
them to come on. Tae and Charlene ran across the lot and then the
road to link up with Nikki.

"Was it good bitch, you just smilin' and shit? Spill the details,"
Nikki teased, hitting her on her arm.

"Fuck yeah it was good! I heard the bitch screamin' outside. He
was murdering that pussy. Shitttt, almost made me flex my own
shit while I was waiting, real talk," Tae joked.

They all was laughing and hi-fiving one another as Marco's
headlights came rolling by. His window was already down so he

was able to talk without stopping. It was illegal for cars to stop on the road or talk to the inmates.

"Goodnight ladies, good looking out. I love you Lena baby, call me later."

With that he disappeared down the road and into the distance.

"You sucked the shit outta that niggah dick didn't you bitch? You see that niggah swerving down the road," Nikki teased.

"Ion't know about all that," Tae objected. "But he bust them guts open fo' sho with all that juice wetting up the back of them shorts. Bitch you betta sneak in the side door between us so I can block that shit cause them flood gates is open."

Charlene made it back to the room safely and as they stood for count, Nikki told her Marco had sent her a text.

Can't wait till next time. That shit felt magical!!

"I told you, don't no niggah want his pussy runnin' rampant!"

Charlene smiled and flicked her off.

"This pussy ain't runnin' nowhere, he made sure of that."

Tae had become one of the sought after studs on the compound; gifts left on her bed, letters underneath her pillow and some women simply bold enough to come to her room wearing nothing but a blanket. Although Bright Eyes tried to make it known on the compound that she and Tae were an item, Tae never confirmed to anyone including Bright Eyes that she was off the market. Yes, she fucked Bright Eyes on a regular but outside of Kelly, Tae held no loyalty for any woman.

Bright Eyes was a little too immature for Tae's taste, especially for Tae to claim as her lady but sexually, she turned Tae on. She had nastiness about her in bed that drove Tae insane. Most women were laid back in bed; made her do all the work but not Bright Eyes. She was so into the groove; she moved, she moaned, she talked dirty, she was open to try anything and most importantly she never denied Tae sex; whether mad, sad or glad, she was always open to give Tae what she wanted and she was same way every time… freaky, Tae liked that.

Bright Eyes also took very good care of Tae. She washed her clothes, took turns with Meko's girl cleaning their room, she did the commissary shopping every week, making sure that Tae had everything she wanted and she cooked every night if Tae didn't like what the kitchen served for dinner.

She was young so Tae tried to understand the childish actions she often displayed. Coming in from work one day, Tae came up the opposite West area stairwell because she was leaving Shawna's room picking up a package. Shawna had suggested that Tae take the West stairwell claiming the East was being waxed but what she wanted was Tae to find something interesting that was happening in the stairwell.

As she rounded the second level of the stairwell, there was Bright Eyes and two other females standing in the clear paned twelve squared metal framed window, wearing nothing but a towel. The men's rec yard was less than eighty feet away just past the fence and they had front row seats to the performances the women were putting on for them. At any given moment you could find a woman or two, dancing, stripping or even making out with one another in the windows. The men watched in amazement, some even standing at the gate jacking off for the ladies in return.

Communication with the men at the FMC often began and continued through letters wrapped around a rock being hurled over the fence containing name, contact information and specific meeting times at the window for a little sexual pleasure.

When Tae saw Bright Eyes she stood back and watched for a few minutes. She wasn't knocking what she was doing because she understood that the women did it to pass the time and Tae knew Bright Eyes was still very much attracted to men, so it wasn't the fact that she was doing it that made Tae say something to her, it was the fact that she wasn't getting anything in return for doing it; nothing other than the sight of a few nigga's private parts, that not only she was seeing but anyone else who just happened to be looking out their room windows.

Tae looked strangely at the creature she come to really like, playing in her mommy; bending over against the window. When Bright Eyes caught a glimpse of Tae out the corner of her eye standing there, she jumped down and tried to cover herself. The other two women were chuckling amongst one another, hoping they were about to see some drama go down.

"If it don't make dollars, it damn sho' don't make sense," Tae told her, continuing on her way up the stairs.

Bright Eyes hurried over to her.

"I... I... I was... I was umm…"

115

"Oh I saw what you were doin' lil' momma, my eyes work very well. Aye do yo' thang baby, you ain't my property. I don't own you baby, you can do whatever you like. You wanna give them niggas something to flick they dicks too, do that… but learn to use what you got to yo' advantage. Don't jack them nigga's dick fo' them, make 'em work for every stroke."

Bright Eyes looked down to the floor.

"It was just a lil' fun, that's all."

"Nah, that kind of fun should be financial… financial gain. Niggah ain't gone buy no milk when the muthafuckin' cow free. They wanna see that pussy, make 'em drop them dollars on yo' books or betta yet, tell him he needs to arrange a package to be dropped off for you. I'll set it up and all you gotta do is relay the details over to him and keep him motivated with your version of a little fun. Let's make a come up off these niggas hard on's… feel me? But wrap this session up cause I'm hungry and they havin' that nasty ass meatloaf today. I want some fried rice aight?"

Bright Eyes shook her head. She'd do anything Tae asked of her.

"And bring that with you," she said smacking Bright Eyes on the ass.

Soon Bright Eyes, with Tae as Puppet Master pulling her strings, mastered the game Tae had taught her. She began using, building a concocted relationship with them, pledging her undying love to them and then getting them to have someone on the outside to bring her packages down to the bottom of the hill. Bright Eyes figured the harder she hustled for Tae and got her packages in, the less Tae needed Shawna around.

Bright Eyes was taking control of what she wanted and what she wanted was Tae. The only woman she knew she had to stand down for was over 200 miles away, Kelly. At first it was difficult for

116

Bright Eyes to see Tae with Kelly at visits. She would stand in her window, watching them in the wooden fenced area with picnic tables set up all around and a beautiful array of flowers planted by the inmate landscaping crew.

Clearly Bright Eyes understood that Tae's heart lie with Kelly but in some ways, she also felt that Kelly took back seat to her as well because she was getting a piece of Tae that even Kelly for the moment, could only dream about.... intimacy.

Despite how she flirted and clowned around on the compound, Bright Eyes knew she was the only one Tae was touching. Any and everything Tae asked her to do sexually, she obliged. Their sexual ora's collided in ways that both knew was untouchable.

Tae had made a jailhouse strap on from Maxi pads and Ace bandages. She took three Maxi pads and stuck them together, wrapped an Ace bandage around them for stiffness, then took a pair of latex gloves and placed them over the bandage. She tied the base of the gloves to another bandage she wrapped around her thighs and waist. The handmade dildo was stiff enough to expand her walls but soft enough not to scratch her flesh and Tae was a master at using it. She worked Bright Eyes from behind or laying on her back on the bed with her legs in the air.

Pounding away at her body, she was able to keep Bright Eyes in line. Stroke by stroke, she filled her head with empty promises and bullshit lines to keep Bright Eyes by her side but in her place. She fucked her against the wall, wrapping her hand around her throat and calling her a nasty bitch.

"You like showin' them niggas yo' pussy don't you? You wishin' they could come up in here and fuck you like this huh? Give you that real dick?"

"No baby, you fuck me just fine."

117

"That's what the fuck is wrong with you now," she said, throwing Bright Eyes upper body on the top of the locker.

Tae watched as Bright Eyes arched her back and began to move her ass in a way that she knew drove Tae up the wall. She reached back and placed her finger inside her ass.

"Yeah, I'm going up in that. When you gone be ready to gimme that ass?"

"I stay ready," she told her grinding her hips back against Tae.

Tae had orgasms from mental pleasure and for her it was better than any physical one she could experience. To watch someone, literally watch someone and it turn you on to the point your body reacts with sexual release, was magical to her.

"I love you Tae… I love you so much."

Tae paused for a moment, telling herself not to makes waves. That if she responded in any way, Bright Eyes would take it to a level all of its own. Faster and faster Bright Eyes threw her ass up against Tae and the more she bounced it rubbed the knot on the latex glove up against Tae's clit. Bright Eyes knew exactly what was happening as she felt Tae's hand grip her waist tighter and her breathing get stronger.

"No, stop."

Tae look up at her and asked her what was wrong.

"I'm tired of us not being able to cum together. I found a way we can."

"Oh really and how is that," Tae asked her, panting.

"Take that off'" she told Tae, climbing on Tae's top bunk.

118

When Tae climbed up on the bunk, Bright Eyes was lying on her stomach. She instructed Tae to lie down on top of her, spread her lips and rest her clit inside the crease of her ass. Tae did as she was instructed and lay her body down on top of her. Bright Eyes began to pull her hips forward which pulled at Tae's clit. She had never felt flesh against her clit before other than her own fingers. She was also the dominant one and in her mind, she wasn't supposed to concentrate on her body, but the body of the one she was loving. Yet here was Bright Eyes once again taking her to a sexual cliff she never been too before and the feeling it gave her made her want to jump off with no parachute.

The feel of her ass muscles rotating underneath her, the yanking of her clit by her ass cheeks, the sound of her voice talking a load of shit in her ear pushed Tae over the cliff.

"Tell me you love me, Tae," she said pulling her muscles tighter, then pushing her ass up against Tae's body to open her cheeks and release her clit only to grip it again with a death grip. "Tell me."

"I love you baby, I love you... fuccckkkkkk.... I love the fuck outta you," Tae moaned as her body began to jerk and spasms. It was the most intense orgasm she'd every experienced because it was ripped from inside her and she had absolutely no control over it.

She rolled over onto her side and tried to regain her composure.

"Where the fuck you learn that shit?"

"Don't matter; I'm that Bitch, I keep tellin' you."

"You are definitely that," she said, smacking Bright Eyes on the ass. "My Bitch."

"You know it baby."

Tae sat up, looked at her watch and noticed the time. She had to get outside and link up with Nikki so she could watch for Tae as she went down the hill to pick up a package. While Bright Eyes focused so hard on Shawna, she hadn't noticed the sexual tension building between Tae and Nikki. Tae laughed to herself as she thought back to her first day on the compound and she met Nikki. Bright Eyes had just flipped out over Shawna asking her to come outside and smoke and when she had stormed out of Tae's room, Nikki had appeared.

"Sounds like you got a firecracker on your hands," she said laughing.

"She aight, just on one, you know how that goes."

"Don't I ever… Nikki, you?"

Nikki had taken Tae around and showed her the compound, introduced her to her friends and gave her the in and outs of the compound; who she should stay away from, who dry snitched, which staff members were cool and who was assholes. Tae asked Nikki about Shawna.

"She a lifer and a pill head but she can get you pretty much anything you need. She has made a lot of friends but also a lot of enemies so you just gotta be careful how you deal with her. When bitches see she feelin' you they'll set some bullshit in motion against you just to fuck wit' her. She aight as a person though, so you just gotta take it fo' what it's worth."

"And what about you Ms. Nikki?"

"What about me?"

"What's up with you?"

"I'm just me. I don't change; I'm the same 24/7."

"Tae, you ready to fill out these slips?" Bright Eyes asked approaching them from behind.

Tae turned, looked at Bright Eyes and then back to Nikki.

"And that is what I don't do Boo… catch you later," Nikki told her, walking off to meet up with her Bunkie Charlene sitting at the table.

Tae and Nikki had become close friends over the months and they watched each other's backs but underneath, through the flirtations and teasing, Tae was developing a real crush on Nikki and as always she was just waiting on the perfect moment to shoot her jumper.

She looked down to Bright Eyes still lying on her stomach, moaning from the pleasure of the experience.

"I gotta go wait on this package."

Bright Eyes lay in Tae's bed, on cloud nine as she watched her dressed. Tae had told her that she loved her and nothing could ruin this moment for her, not even the face that suddenly appeared in the doorway after Tae jumped off the bunk to answer the knock.

"Let's go bitch," Nikki told her, looking up to Bright Eyes on the bed and then to Tae.

"Do you need to shower first? Ion't want that shit blowin' in the wind all in my face and shit."

Tae laughed as they exited the room and Bright Eyes rolled her eyes.

"Bitch," she spat out.

She knew Nikki like so many other didn't like her simply because she was the one on Tae's side, not them. She wanted so bad to rid her life of them one by one and after the words Tae had just whispered in her ear so powerfully, Bright Eyes planned to do just that.

Over the next 60 days, Mel had become Connor's sexual fixation and he had become Mel's heart. For as long as she could remember, men had wanted her body and were willing to pay her handsomely for it but during those encounters, the words they spoken were clearly limited to the *feel* of her body. Connors was different in the way that he spoke to her inner beauty as a woman; he spoke to her soul. He told her how his thoughts were so consumed with images of her; of how when he lay with his wife he often thought of their sexual escapades in order to get off.

Mel, never really having a real relationship before in her life, began to mistake what was clearly lust for love. Constantly she found herself day dreaming about him as she once again watched the hours on her white Fossil watch tick by until his shift had arrived.

Connors was truly infatuated with Mel also. He had experienced things with her that he'd never experienced with any woman before. He was such an attractive man and yes, women came on to him all the time; co-workers, at church, at the gym and of course the other inmates on the compound flirted with him constantly. Connors however was very protective of his life at home. He dared mess around with someone who could possibly run into him with his wife at the Wal-Mart one day. His wife was an upstanding member of their church and small knit community. Despite his actions inside the compound, he respected her enough not to give any woman on the "outside" the ups on her.

So at home he was forced to play by the rules of the good husband; smoldering the desires burning inside him to explore his sexual fantasies but Mel gave him the opportunity to be free by open invitation. She ignited the flame inside him that he had forced to lie dormant for so many years and for that burning flame, he gave her anything she wanted; money, jewelry, perfume and even sent money home to her mother a few times to help with the care of her brother and sisters. There were suspicions by the other inmates that they were involved but no one had any solid proof.

In prison, just as it was on the streets, if you were seen talking to someone more than once it was automatically assumed that you were sleeping together and because they were good at playing the roles of officer and inmate when necessary, it opened the way for the better roles of secret lovers whenever possible. It seemed to Mel that Connors spent his free time at home watching porno's, getting ideas that he then took out on her when the opportunity presented itself; new positions he wanted to try and of course she didn't mind. Mel just wanted him in any fashion she could have him.

Over the course of two months Mel had opened her body and soul to him along with every avenue of pleasure her body could offer. She had gotten lost in the rules of her own upbringing; never allow business to mix with pleasure. Mel however hadn't come after him for business, this was all pleasure and the more she felt him, felt his want and need for her, the more she let her guard down and fell for him.

It made her feel good not to simply be looked at as a piece of meat for sale and although he did things for her financially, in her own mixed up way, Mel figured that since she had seduced him, the circumstance surrounding their affair was very different from the clients she once served on the streets.

With soft innuendos of love in her ear, Mel truly believed that Connors had those same feelings for her. That he needed her for completion; completion of what his wife couldn't offer him and that she along with the confinement of the camp provided him a safe haven of freedom... free to be as nasty as he wanted to be... free to be himself.

For the most part she was correct, the confinement of the compound allowed him the openness to explore but what Mel soon found out was that exploration can be an adventure deemed more exciting the more paths you have available to explore. Over the past two weeks, Mel began to notice that Connors had been holding more and more conversation with another inmate named Kieara. Short, dark skinned with natural hair that she kept braided up into a big poof ponytail, Kieara was pretty Mel had to admit and she could tell by the way Connors responded to her that he indeed thought so too. She knew that look on his face all too well.

He only had a few more weeks left on this rotation and Mel was not about to let Kieara horn in on her territory. Not just because of the financial benefits he brought to the table but the fact she cared for him very deeply and from the countless whispers he'd planted in her ear, she knew he cared for her as well.

As Mel waited impatiently for the usual time they met up to arrive, she lay on her bunk listening to her headphones. She wanted, no she needed to know if Connors had any interest in Kieara and she planned on finding out. One thing she learned from her dealings with Brian was her directness and her boldness. He'd also taught her that a closed mouth led to starvation.

The minutes seemed to tick by so slowly as she sighed deeply; allowing her mind to imagine the worst. She needed to see him, touch him, and put the insecurities she felt overtaking her to rest. She needed to be in his arms, needed him to confirm his desire and want for her and only her.

"... tell me it's real, the feeling that I feel, tell me that it's real. Don't let love come to just pass us by. Try is all we have to do; it's up to me and you, to make this special love last forever more..."

The time had finally arrived and Mel climbed down from her bunk and headed down the darkened hallway. As she approached the opening where the hallway met the lobby, she looked over at the officer's station. The door was closed. Mel removed her house shoes, picked them up off the floor and tip-toed barefooted over to the red metal door. Gently she leaned against the coldness of the metal, pressing her ear against it to see if she could hear anything coming from inside but all was quiet.

She went back to the hallway opening and looked down both ways to see if anyone was coming before she walked to the door, kneeled down onto the floor and peeked underneath the bottom to see if she could see any movement through the tiny slit. Mel's stomach became queasy as it became apparent to her that Connors was elsewhere on the compound.

She put on her shoes and walked back down the hallway to her room. She tried lying down on her bunk, thinking he'd pass by soon enough, flashing his flashlight in her face like always when he did his rounds. He was also a smoker she reminded herself, he could be outside. Yet the longer she lay there, staring out the metal framed window the more her gut instincts told her that the man she loved was somewhere with another woman and she fully intended to find out if her woman's intuition was correct.

Mel climbed back down from the bed, slipped on a pair of her sweats over her shorts, pulled on her sweatshirt, threw on her tennis shoes then grabbed her cigarettes and lighter. She headed down the hallway, around the corner and out the side of the building towards the pavilion.

She lit her cigarette and looked down at her watch. *2:04am*, plenty of time to do what he would normally be doing with her before 4am count. Mel was becoming more aggravated the more she stood there and allowed all the possibilities to creep into her mind; where he could be, what he could be doing and more importantly who he could be doing it with.

There were two other inmates out underneath the pavilion so Mel took the opportunity to question them concerning Connors whereabouts.

126

"Not since I seen him upstairs talking to KeKe in the laundry room," One of the women answered. "And you know how she is so ain't no telling where they ass at."

Mel began to feel sick, her palms becoming sweaty, her heart racing; light headed thinking of the first time she met up with Connors in the laundry... the conversation, the flirting, the sexual teasing back and forth and ultimately his dick ended up in her hand. More so she thought of what it led to.

Mel flicked the cigarette butt onto the ground and headed back inside the building. She ran up the back steps as quietly as she could, heart pounding inside her chest, afraid of what she may find once she reached the small room. As she approached the door she thought she was going to faint. She stopped one room short of the doorway but when she noticed the laundry room door was opened, she gathered herself and kept moving. He wouldn't be that careless.

She walked around to the stairwell that led down to the basement. She was determined to check the camp from top to bottom, looking in every spot they had been known to frequent together. Mel headed to the Rec room first, again leaning in and listening at the door for sounds of movement before opening the

When she didn't see him, she moved on to the Rec closest, equipment room, fitness room and the opposite basement stairwell before heading back up to the first floor. Walking down the hallway her emotions finally began to settle; thinking that maybe she had just over reacted and had allowed jealousy to consume her. After all, hadn't he told her that she was the source of his fantasies? That she not Kieara was his first and final thought of the day? She almost laughed at the silliness she felt for running around like a crazy woman. She decided to head back outside for another cigarette before heading back to her room.

As she passed by Mrs. Crumple's office she caught the light from outside the window flicker across a shiny object in the window. She walked past the door, ducked down and squatted back past it. Once on the other side of the door she stood up against the wall and told herself to walk away.

Don't look in there Mel, just keep going.

She couldn't; she had to know. She peeked her head inside the window quickly and pulled it back. She couldn't make out exactly what she'd seen so she did it again and again, she saw the light flicker against the shiny object. She pulled once more, knowing it was flickering against something familiar to her, his name tag.

Mel turned her stomach from against the wall and turned onto her side looking into the office. Leaning back against the wall was Connors with his hands balled inside Kieara's ponytail, guiding her head back and forth across his jimmy. Kieara had her palms against his thighs as Connors rest his head back against the concrete. She could only see the side view of his face with hers pressed against the glass but she could tell he was enjoying the feeling Kieara was giving him.

Mel felt a tear roll down her face as she pushed back away from the door.

How could he do this to me? I thought he cared about me, how could he hurt me like this?

Mel felt the hurt transcend from zero to off the charts within sixty seconds and before she knew it, she hit the door with her fist causing the occupants inside to jump. When she realized what she had done, she took off running down the hallway, rushing back to her room. She quickly took off her shoes, sweatshirt and pants. She jumped up the ladder, threw her headphones on and turned her back to the doorway. She had so many emotions running through her.

She was hurt and angered by his actions, saddened by the games he played with her feelings and disappointed that he'd felt the need to go to someone else to fulfill his desires. Mel couldn't breathe. She had more questions than answers and she wasn't sure if she wanted to know. Mel had never felt the pain of rejection before. From the moment Brian had touched her on the couch back in the projects; Mel had controlled what she wanted with her body. She didn't know how to handle the fact that someone else had the power to not only do the same but take something of her in the process.

As she lay there listening to music she stared out at the moonlight as the tears fell from the bridge of her nose down onto the white pillowcase below.

"... love has finally come at last and I'm never gonna give it back... oh no no no... it's like an omen said, one that simply read, you can't miss what you never had. I thought that love was just a feeling, that I'd give to him and in return he'd give it back..."

Mel felt her core shake as she fought to hold it together. She hadn't cried when she caught her case, when she got sentenced nor when she had gotten separated from her siblings who had meant the world to her. How had she allowed this situation to get the best of her? How had she allowed him to invade her life and take over it the way he had?

She became angry at herself for letting her guard down; knowing she had no business going against the grain of her world. She wanted to hit him, spit on him, destroy him but she also wanted him to hold her, tell her he was sorry and that he would never hurt her again.

She would get her chance as she faintly heard his keys jingling in the distance; he was doing rounds. Mel wiped her face and quickly turned to face the doorway, pretending to be asleep. Connors needed to find out who was out of their bunks so he could narrow down who may have knocked on the door and caught him in a very compromising position. A position that in the wrong hands could cost him his career among other things.

As he approached Mel's room, she tried her best to control her sniffling. Connors stopped in front of her room and shined the light into her face causing Mel to shy away from its brightness. He gripped his keys to silence then as he headed over to her bunk. He rubbed her face with his fingers and Mel jerked away at the thought of him touching her after he had just touched Kieara.

"Wake up, wake up baby," he whispered, shaking her on her hips. "Meet me downstairs in the Rec room in ten minutes," he told her.

Mel wanted to kick him in the face and tell him to go to hell but as he rubbed her arm all she could muster up to say was a soft, *okay.*

As Connors finished rounds, he took mental notes of who was not in their room and if after speaking with Mel, finding that it wasn't her who had seen him with Kieara, he knew who to begin conversation with for information. Passing Kieara's room, she sprang to the doorway.

"All clear?" she asked him, hoping to get another piece of him.

"Maybe another night. Let things calm down first."

A disappointed Kieara went back inside her room and got into bed. She wanted to get her hooks into him and she like many including Mel was willing to do anything to do so. Kieara knew that he had something going with Mel; she couldn't prove it and she also didn't care. She knew that if given the opportunity she could take him from Mel and that she planned to do.

Mel waited inside the Rec room unsure of how she'd react or what she's say once Connors entered. She sat down on the ledge of the pool table and when she heard the keys coming down the stairs she began to feel uneasy all over again.

Connors entered the Rec room, stood just inside the doorway and stared at her.

"You got anything you wanna tell me?" he asked her, prying to see if it was her at the office door.

"I should be askin' you that right? You got something you wanna tell me? Like was it good to you? That bitch on her knees for you? You grabbin' her ponytail and shit? Like did she suck yo' dick better than me cause from the looks of it, she was doin' a damn good job."

Mel felt herself getting angry and Connors saw it too. He knew that he'd better put out this fire brewing and quick. He had to calm her, reassure her that it was simply a mistake and wheel her back in before she went off half-cocked and did something out of anger that they'd both regret later.

"It wasn't…."

"What it looked like? Really? Cause to me it looked like she was on her knees with her hands on your thighs while your dick was in her mouth. That's not what it was?"

Connors tried to touch her but Mel pulled away and that bothered him.

"Baby, baby, baby, stop it… ok yeah, that's all it was, some head. She been coming at me, beginning to suck my dick so I just finally gave in. It was no big deal."

"No big deal? I'm glad you see my feelings as no big fuckin' deal! Tell me if you walked in somewhere and saw me sucking some muthafucka's dick or some niggah fuckin' me, would it still be no big deal?"

Connors grabbed Mel by the legs on the pool table and yanked her close to him.

"You don't mean that. Fuck yeah it would be a big deal. I'd lose my fuckin' mind. How could you think I don't care about yo' feelings? I let the bitch suck my dick, that's all. I ain't fuck the bitch and I damn shol' ain't do this," he said, throwing her back onto the table.

He ripped her shorts down her legs, spread them as wide as they could go and rush her mommy in desperation. Fiercely he tore away at her lips with his mouth and tongue. Mel began to struggle to get away, not from anger but from the pleasure. He put everything he had into sucking her mommy and Mel was losing her mind. He came up for air only to talk to her.

"I told you, you my bitch. I wouldn't suck another woman's pussy. This pussy fills me up. I let her suck my dick, that ain't shit. This right here, this intimate shit... this that shit that matter," he said, swallowing her inside his mouth, the roughness from his stubby beard brushing against her skin.

"You my fantasy, you my world... nobody but you. You shouldn't care if a bitch on her knees for me as long as I'm on my knees for you, feel me?" he said, unzipping his pants.

He removed his hardness from his boxers and told Mel to put on her headphones, close her eyes and allow him to take her to Heaven. He shoved his jimmy inside her as she placed her headphones on her ears and lay back against the green felt of the pool table.

His movements were intense and Mel closed her eyes as she felt her insides adjust to the hardness of his jimmy.

"... girl you know that I'm committed to someone else, so why you wanna push me to the limit? Every time that I come near you. I wanna do what you want me to do but it wouldn't be cool. You know I want to kiss you but I'd better leave now, I want to stay here all night but I need to go. You make me weak so while I'm strong, I'd better leave well enough alone..."

Mel felt her pressure build along with him swelling inside her. Dee Harvey serenaded her as she grabbed the back of his head; him towering above her as they both came in unison. He lay down on top of her, kissing her with a passion Mel knew he couldn't fake. He told her he was sorry.

"I'll never let another suck this dick again, it's yours, it's all yours baby."

Mel heard the words she needed to hear and just that quickly put the thoughts of Kieara from her head. Kieara however, Mel would soon come to find was the least of her worries. Something else was brewing on the horizon. Something she never saw coming.

Shawna stood at the entrance of the officer's station and as she leaned up against the wooden red door, she looked over at Tae who was among the many curious faces trying to find out what was going on with her.

Shawna was handcuffed, which at the camp usually meant that a trip to the county jail was on its way. Inmates could be sent to county for various reasons but mostly depended upon the level of the write up you received... fighting, getting involved with an officer, disrespecting staff or getting caught with contraband being the biggest ones.

Shawna's room had been the target of a shakedown that morning with every inch being searched with a magnifying glass and photographed after an anonymous note was placed under Ms. Harlett's, the camp administrator's door informing her that Shawna had received a package in through her visit the day before containing pills, weed and jewelry.

Every letter, true or not that threatened the security of the compound had to be taken serious per prison policy and investigated. It was at the camp administrator's discretion if the inmate in question would be packed out sent to the county lock up pending the investigation. This wasn't the case for Shawna who now had tears falling down her face. An investigation wasn't needed as the searching officer's found the Oxycodone in the prescription pills bottle, the jewelry and weed stashed in separate poles of her off white metal bed frame. A search of Shawna's puke green colored mattress also revealed a slit that led the way down into the foam that hid her stash of cell phones.

The information on the letter was very detailed. It told the officer's exactly where to look and once Shawna saw them lift her bed frame and dig up into one of its posts, she knew that someone she dealt with on an up close and personal level had betrayed her.

Shawna stood at the door, watching one of the officer's walk past her with all of her things into three huge clear plastic trash bags. Seeing an inmate get packed out didn't necessarily mean they weren't returning, it just meant the camp wasn't about to hold the bed open in their absence.

Yet, with them finding the Oxycodone alone both Shawna and Tae knew this would be the last time they laid eyes on one another for Shawna would be getting shipped to an FCI behind the gates. The fact that she was a lifer and probably wouldn't have additional charges added to her case did little to comfort Shawna as she mouthed the question to Tae leaning up against the wall.

"Tell me you didn't?"

Tae shook her head no.

"Never," she said, running her finger up the inside of her arm, tracing a vein, indicating that snitching wasn't in her blood.

But the person standing next to her, leaning against Tae's shoulder was enjoying the moment, knowing it had come with just a few strokes of her ink pen. Bright Eyes had slipped the note under Ms. Harlett's door the night before after she'd seen something transpire between Shawna and Tae she didn't appreciate.

She and Tae had just had words concerning Bright Eyes inability to get in a package that Tae desperately needed to get to someone who was offering to pay a hefty price to obtain it.

"You so busy tryin' to lay under me all the time, you slippin' on what you suppose to be doin' We handle business first remember? That comes before anything... fucking, love or lust."

135

Bright Eyes wasn't slippin'; truth was she was simply tired of dealing with the men across the way. The game had lost its luster and the more she had of Tae, the more she wanted. Toying with the men, Tae's benefit or not had become lame to her. All she wanted was Tae and so she began lying about the men being unable to get packages in for her, claiming they were either on restriction or lock down.

"Look baby, I been tryin' and I can't do anything about what them niggas got going on. So why you comin' at me like that. Tell one of them lil' clucks you be dealin' with on the sly to get it in for you."

Tae raised her eyes brow to Bright Eyes and without even responding, walked out the room and despite Bright Eyes calling behind her, kept walking until she reached Shawna's door. Bright Eyes knew she had pull her foot in her mouth as Tae had given her the respect of not dealing with Shawna as long as Bright Eyes could get in for her what she needed. She followed behind Tae and once she saw the door close to Shawna's room, she took a few steps back and dipped into a neighboring room, watching for the square shaped reflection of the light to appear on the wall across from her. This would let her know that Shawna had removed the bathrobe from her door window.

She stood there for what felt like hours and once she saw the light's reflection appear on the wall she waited for the door to open. She peeked her head around the corner just enough to see the opening of the doorway but remain unseen… at least that what she thought.

As Tae turned to the left to walk away, Shawna looked to the right at caught a quick glimpse of Bright Eyes peeking around the door frame. Shawna decided to give her something to see since she was stalking them. She called after Tae and walked out the room. She walked around to Tae's front side; leaving Tae's back turned to Bright Eyes. Shawna grabbed Tae by the light grey t-shirt and pulled her close to her. She glanced at the doorway from which Bright Eyes was lurking before she placed a kiss on Tae's lips; her eyes never leaving Bright Eye's direction.

Tae looked at Shawna, wiping the corners of her mouth. Shawna said no words; she simply walked back into her room and closed her door as Tae confusingly continued up the hallway and then the stairs. Once she saw Tae disappear, Bright Eyes left the room and walked up to Shawna's room door. She thought of going inside and confronting her but once she stepped up onto her tippy toes and saw Shawna putting her weed up into the bed rails, she had a better idea. One that would rid her of the impending threat of Shawna for good.

She proceeded upstairs to her dorm room, grabbed a pad of paper from her locker along with a pen and hopped up onto her top bunk. She wrote down exactly what she knew was in the room and embellished the rest with what she had heard Shawna was capable of getting in. Bright Eyes knew that the officer's didn't just check once place during shake downs but would tear the room apart so she knew they'd eventually find the rest of whatever she was hiding.

"You hoes gon' learn to stop fuckin' with me." she said to herself as she slid the folded piece of notebook paper underneath the office door then took off because she heard voices in the distance.

She smirked as stood next to Tae, pretending to be toying with the chipping nail polish from her fingers. Shawna looked at Bright Eyes whose eyes stayed focused downward. She had no proof but she knew somehow she'd had a hand in what was happening to her she just didn't know how. Shawna was very careful in who she allowed in her business, especially the part that jeopardized her livelihood. Yet the smirk Bright Eyes was attempting to conceal on her face told her gut that she was right.

As they led Shawna out of the camp door, Tae felt a sense of uneasiness. She couldn't explain it but something just didn't feel right to her. It was the same feeling she had the night she was in the car with Charlotte and ignoring it that time, had landed her in prison. This time she told herself she would get to the bottom of it. Maybe it was just the reality that you could be caught breaking the rule in such a relaxed environment, she thought to herself. A reality she herself wasn't ready to take on. If she couldn't be close to Kelly and have her visits she didn't know what she would do.

"Maybe that's a sign it's time fo' a niggah to chill out."

A week and a half had passed since Shawna had left and Tae was getting more and more orders in. She was starting to think that maybe Shawna had just become careless or trusted the wrong person and that's what got her caught up. Yet while Tae was planning on how she could keep her fate different from Shawna's a letter arrived for her at mail call.

It was addressed from an Indiana address and Tae had no idea who it could be from but once she began reading it, it quickly became clear.

>   *Tae,*
>
>   *You know I wouldn't for a second think that you were behind me getting caught up. I'm being shipped out to the FCI in Florida within the next few weeks which is fucked up because I'll be so far away from my husband and family.*
>
>   *I'm just writing to tell you to watch yo' back with ole girl. Something you should know... the night you came to my room for that package, ya girl was in the room next door, peeking around the frame. That's why I walked in the hallway and kissed you because she was straight on some lurkin' shit. The next day I'm bein' shook down. Too much of a funkin' coincidence for me!*

I can't prove it was her but I'm no fuckin' fool. Watch ya'self and keep in touch. The address on the front is my moms. She'll get a letter to me.

Shawna

Tae read the letter over and over again. Could Bright Eyes in one of her jealousy rants really do something like that? Maybe she was mistaken, knowing Bright Eyes didn't care for her but Tae couldn't see her doing something of this magnitude to ruin someone's life like this. That was until she brought it to Bright Eyes. point blank that evening and asked her if she had indeed snitched on Shawna.

"What you mad? The bitch stepped in waters she couldn't swim in and thought the shit was cute until the bitch needed a life jacket and found out she ain't have one."

Tae looked at Bright Eyes becoming more furious by the second.

"Fuck you mean water she couldn't swim in? Why the fuck would do that? You are fuckin' outta control with this dumb shit! Do you know what the fuck you did to that woman? You sent her way the fuck to Florida. That fuckin' far away from her family, away from her husband next door and all her friends. Just because you don't got nobody comin' to see you and yo' family is on some real fuck you shit; don't give you the fuckin' right! On some old possessive stupid shit? I can't fuckin' believe yo' dumb ass!"

"Why you clowning over a bitch you claim you don't give a fuck about? You think I care about her damn husband or her fuckin' family? Tae you kissed that bitch, I saw it with my own eyes! You think I give a fuck about her?"

"What?" Tae said, moving to within inches of her face. "I ain't kiss no fuckin' body. She kissed me cause she knew yo' immature ass was looking from the room next door ole' dumb ass lil' girl!

139

Do you know what the fuck coulda happened behind this shit? You ain't think about the fact that she coulda easily have told them about me and what I do. You an insane muthafucka runnin' around here half cocked over some bullshit."

Tae mashed Bright Eyes in the face and she fell down onto Meko's bed.

"Stupid bitch, stay the fuck away from me. I can't take you serious right now. I can't trust you. Sneaking around setting muthafucka's up and shit. How the fuck I know I ain't next?"

Bright Eyes began to cry as she reached out for Tae.

"Bae I would never, never do anything to hurt you. I'm sorry. I ain't know you was gone flip like this but that bitch... that bitch was being just a little too disrespectful to me... to us!"

"Us? What the fuck I keep telling you about that us shit? Don't no muthafucka owe you fuckin' respect! Every muthafucka on this compound know I gotta gal at home, you think they give a fuck about you?"

"Oh so because I'm not your precious Kelly, I don't deserve to be respected? Fuck that, that bi..."

Tae towered above her, grabbing her hair in the top of her head.

"Fuck you say? What you call her? Don't get fucked up!"

Nikki hearing the commotion next door ran into the room and pulled Tae off of Bright Eyes and out into the hallway.

"The fuck is wrong with you? I know you ain't about to go down over this crazy hoe!"

"That bitch snitched on Shawna! Dumb ass coulda got all us fucked up."

Nikki shook her head.

"Damn that's fucked up but Shawna a big girl, she knew the risks. You going to county ain't gone make shit no better. You need to leave that lil girl alone. Separate yo 'self from her and stop dealin' with her before she make you fuck off what time you have left."

Tae turned to Bright Eyes who was wiping her face.

"Aey, get the fuck out my room!"

Bright Eyes whimpered as she walked by Tae and Nikki then stopped.

"I'm the one here with you Taedra! I'm the one getting this shit in for you, showing my body and shit to get you what the fuck you need, not Kelly, me!"

Tae reached for Bright Eyes and Nikki jumped between them.

"Just gone somewhere lil girl before you get hurt now," Nikki told her, pointing down the hallway.

"Naw, I'm done being the one gettin' hurt... believe that! I thought I just proved that," she spit out as she turned to walk off.

Nikki told Tae to let it go.

"We gotta party to go to after count tonight, fuck that bitch. You need to get yo' mind right. Let's go outside."

Tae and Nikki headed down the back stairwell and Nikki looked at Tae and laughed.

141

"I told you that he was crazy didn't I? Yo' ass betta put in a slip to move downstairs or somethin' and get away from that bitch. Shhittttt you see she spend all day Sunday's watching Snapped and shit. Betta not eat none of that hoe's cookin' that's fo' damn sho'; ass gone be eatin' some of these rats runnin' round downstairs!"

When Nikki and Charlene stood for 4pm count, Tucker walked past their room. Back on shift for the third rotation in Charlene's final eighteen months, he had made it a very painful experience. Charlene didn't know that he had read her letter about Marco's visit until his next rotation on duty. He had caught her coming out of the shower down the hall from her room and told her it was that time again.

Charlene had tried to lie her way out of meeting up with him by telling him that she wasn't feeling good but Tucker just looked at her and told her, "I got the perfect medicine for you right here my little peach, now be there," he said starting to walk off.

"I can't, I really don't' feel good. Now I realize you could write me up but I don't really care at this point. I'm going to lay down."

Officer Tucker walked back up to Charlene and stopped within inches of her face.

"What did you just say to me you lil' bitch? Write up? Hell I can do so much more than that my dear. I seem to recall a letter you wrote home to your nigger beau, asking him to come meet you at the Rec center for a little freaky rendezvous. I intercepted said letter and made copies of it before I mailed it, ya know for safe keeping and all."

Charlene almost fainted at his words.

"Now how much you wanna bet that if I ask the main office to pull security tape in the Rec center for that month, they'd find you there, bent over getting ass fucked by Mandingo? Now I'm only gone say this one more time, be there right before count."

Charlene felt the inside of her stomach drop. She was so fucking sick of him and everything twisted thing he stood for but she had no choice. If he turned in that letter and had the tape pulled, she could get into so much trouble; trouble not just limited to SHU (time locked in the nearby Lexington county jail's Segregated Housing Unit) but possibly face new charges and be shipped to the nearest FCI, none of which were close to home.

She bit down on the inside of her jaw so hard she thought she'd drew blood. She tried to fight back her tears. She knew she had to give him what he wanted. Out of the three months of his rotations at least once a month, he disgraced her with his poison.

Every night she prayed as her out date drew closer that he wouldn't return but as he winked at her in passing during count time, she knew that prayer had somehow missed God's mailbox. Charlene had been in such good spirits lately, since Marco's first visit to the Rec center, he'd come back once a month to rekindle their sexual flame. In between those visits, she would sneak and call him on the pre-paid phones Tae would get in for them. His conversations sounded like the Marco of old; back when she knew she was the apple of his eye.

Now she was set to go home the next day to be with him and the kids. That prayer she smiled to herself had been answered and there was nothing she would allow to interfere with that. So as she stood staring down at the callout appointment sheet and Tucker approached from behind, instructing her to meet him one last time, she made up in her mind she would make sure he forever remembered her and the hell he took her through simply because he could. He wanted one last hurrah? Well that was exactly what Charlene vowed to give him.

After ten pm count, she reported downstairs to the Rec room broom closet which had become his secret hide away. Unbeknownst to Tucker, Charlene and Nikki had spent the evening hatching the perfect plan, one that Tucker would never see coming.

144

As she stood in the tiny closet leaning back on the rusty white sink, Charlene fought back the tears of shame. Yes she knew she wasn't the only woman in the camp experiencing this disgrace at the hands of Tucker and officers like him but knowing that didn't make it hurt any less.

She looked at the metal mop wringer and for a moment she imagined Tucker's tiny dick being crushed between the rusty blades; her foot applying the pressure. That made her chuckle. But what Nikki had proposed had been brilliant, something to make the compound, the FMC, the Warden and all his staff take notice.

When she heard the door knob turn, Charlene's stomach became nauseated and when she smelled his flesh against her face she fought the overwhelming urge to vomit. Right on schedule as Charlene pushed the slob from her mouth, she heard Nikki's voice in the distance calling for Officer Tucker saying it was about to be a fight on the main level.

"Hurry up and make me cum, I got to go."

Charlene felt him swell and as he seeped out into her mouth, he heard a more urgent scream for him. Tucker knew he had to get upstairs quickly because if in fact it were a fight ensuing and another officer responded and put it out over the radio; he'd have a lot of explaining to do.

The setup was perfect. Nikki had planned it so she could throw Tucker off his game enough to allow Charlene to pull off the stunt of a lifetime. Normally Tucker never allowed Charlene to leave until he checked to make sure she had swallowed his semen but because Nikki was screaming for him, in all the commotion he was too hurried to check.

When he bolted out of the closet, Charlene reached in her pocket, pulled out the tiny clear plastic bag she'd taken from their room,

145

opened it and spit the salty disgusting contents of her mouth into a corner of the bag. She tied it in a knot and rubbed the plastic against the metal mop railing to tear off the excess plastic. She took the small bag and placed it down inside her panties. When she exited the broom closet Charlene had a smirk on her face only Nikki would understand.

"You good boo," she asked her as Charlene entered their room. "Did you get it?"

Charlene closed their room door and placed Nikki's bathrobe over the small window, She pulled the tiny bag from her white cotton underwear, held it up in the air and gave it a little thump with her fingers.

"Yep, I sure in the fuck did!"

They both screamed as Nikki jumped hopped off her bunk and hugged her friend. She pulled her long wavy hair back behind her ear and took the bag from Charlene.

"Ewwww... this shit look like spoiled fuckin' milk," she frowned. "That muthafucka need his nuts checked. I wouldn't impregnate my worst enemy with this nasty lookin' shit. That's probably why yo' edges and shit fallin' out," she teased, trying to keep Charlene's spirits high. She was leaving in the morning going home to her family and that's all Nikki wanted her to focus on.

Nikki placed the bag down inside the red and white mini water cooler. She'd filled it with ice from the kitchen after dinner to keep his semen alive and chilled.

"Now, that's done; bitch go brush so we can get yo' goodbye party started. You know how we do. Meet me downstairs in the pool room," she told Charlene holding up a pint of Vodka she'd had Mr. Woodson, the kitchen supervisor bring in for her.

"How did you...Tae?"

"Not this one, Mr. Woodson. Shit, you ain't think all them sneaky feels on my ass was for nothing did you? Shitt I had to put his crusty ass on payroll."

They laughed.

"Fuck all that, hurry up. It's time to get fuuuuccccckkkeeeeddddd up!"

Charlene shook her head at the crazy chick in front of her. She had come to love her as a sister. She would miss Nikki so much when she headed out in the morning and while Nikki was use to people coming and going, Charlene wasn't used to walking away.

She felt a tear well up in her eyes as she walked to the restroom with her toothpaste and brush.

How can you hurt so much walking outta this place, she wondered but then she thought back to all the pillow talks, all the birthdays, holidays, visits or lack of, letters, pictures, gifts, movies and secrets they had shared over their time together as bunkies.

Charlene realized that no one on the outside actually knew her as well as Nikki did... she developed something on the inside of these walls she had never possessed out on the streets... a true friendship.

As she walked into the pool room in the basement, she wiped her eyes as she took in the atmosphere. All of her acquaintances were there. Nikki had gotten the boom box from the rec room so the party had music, the room was decorated with handmade butterfly decor, her favorite and latex gloves decorated as balloons.

On one side, the pool table was lined with cards and gifts the women either hand-made or purchased from commissary for her to

147

take home with her and on the other side was the food... fried rice, burritos, quesadillas, chicken salad, chips, and both cheese cakes and chocolate Snickers cake made from scratch.

Charlene felt the tears build again. The way you handled your stay, the friends you'd made, the impression you made and the lives you touched while there were all represented in the way they sent you off and Charlene was being sent off in style.

"No crying bitch, we came to party!"

And with the next count not coming until 4am, party they did... dancing, singing, playing spades, dominoes and creeping out to smoke both joints and Black & Milds. Nikki mixed the Vodka with the fruit punch so it wouldn't be so obvious they were drinking. Charlene had no thoughts of the next day; she just enjoyed herself with those who had become a surrogate family to her.

Nikki walked over to her friend and grabbed her hand.

"It ain't over Momma, sit down."

Charlene took a seat in the grey folding chair as Nikki walked over to the radio and turned on the CD. As the bass began to bump from the boom box speakers, the outside rec room door opened and in walked Tae, Meko and Kris... the three baddest studs on the compound, dressed in hand sewn White tuxedos made from bed sheets and material donated to the camp. All three had their hair freshly braided in designer styles, using black yarn braided in for thickness. Crocheted roses were pinned to their tux lapels and fragrance oil had them all smelling good.

"It's getting late, why are you still here girl? Have you made up your mind, you wanna make love tonight? I want you to hold me, I want you to be for real girl, please tonight..."

Tae walked over to Charlene and threw each of her legs on the outside of Charlene's chair and began to grind her hips seductively as she sung to her and Charlene blushed uncontrollably.

"... *don't want you to go, cause I don't feel like being lonely no, not tonight, Lena not tonight....*"

She moon walked over to Nikki who was sitting on the ledge of the pool table watching the performance. She lifted Nikki's legs and wrapped them around her waist and began to pump against her body.

"... *you're so scared, cause I can feel your heartbeat, it's soooooo fast...*"

Tae looked Nikki in the eyes and smiled.

"I'm a get that pussy sooner or later," she whispered in her ear.

Nikki pushed her back towards Charlene and Tae and the crew finished performing for her; caressing, rubbing and putting on a world class show for her. Each gave her the rose from their lapel and a kiss on the lips to end the show. Charlene loved it all.

Nikki began handing her gifts to open; from handmade picture frames to perfume, each gift had sentimental meaning to her however when Nikki placed her gift on Charlene's lap, she too began to feel the overtake her. Was it because she was seeing another friend leave or because once again she was stuck behind, being robbed of freedom once more?

Maybe, Nikki resigned; it was a little bit of both but more so it was because her friend was leaving. Nikki knew all too well from her previous experiences that when women left and got home into the real world, things quickly got busy for them. They had new responsibilities to worry about and soon keeping in touch became a distant memory, not by choice... it was just life sometimes and

Nikki had grown to love the woman before her unlike she'd ever loved anyone she'd met along this journey. She would be so hurt if they lost touch because she would truly miss her.

Charlene opened the taped up decorated box, threw the newspaper from inside onto the floor and pulled out clear trash bag. Inside was a beautiful handmade blanket, made of Charlene's favorite colors with her initials stitched in the middle.

"Oh my God Nikki, it's so beautiful! I saw Kim working on this but I had no idea! Oh my God, I love it and I love you so much! I'll keep it forever Nikki I promise!!"

"Yeah well you'd better and every time you wrapped up watching a movie, think of me, your Bunkie," she said, her voice beginning to crack.

Charlene put the box on the floor and stood up putting her arms around Nikki.

"You not my Bunkie, you not even my friend. You my sister Nikki and I couldn't have made it through any of this without you by my side, you know that. You taught me so much and I'll always, always love you."

They hugged and Tae walked over to the two of them and rubbed both of their backs.

"Damn can I get in the middle of this sandwich?"

That made the women giggle and they pulled Tae into their embrace.

"I love you lil' mamasita's, ya'll know that," Tae told them.

Tae placed a kiss on Charlene's lips and then kissed Nikki on the lips as well.

"Ion't know why ya'll just won't fuck and get that shit out ya'll system," Charlene told them.

They all laughed and for the moment they were able to enjoy themselves again. They would worry about the sadness in the morning… that among other things.

Mel had one woman on the compound she considered herself to be close too. The same woman that had greeted her at the front door when she first hit the compound, Ms. Ella. She had become more a surrogate mother to Mel over the time she had been on the camp grounds. Mel did the things for Ella that she knew was difficult for her to do on her own because of her age and diabetes; laundry, changed her bedding, did her hair for her, went to commissary with her and read her letters from home and her Bible to her because of Ella's failing eyesight.

Mel reminded Ella of her only daughter she had lost early in life to a car accident; determined to take the world by the horns and live life her way and hers alone. Ella saw something inside Mel that Mel didn't see in herself... the beauty of a woman with the heart of God. Ella couldn't understand why Mel allowed herself to be degraded into being Connors' private porno star and why she couldn't see that she deserved so much better than what she was allowing herself to receive in exchange for compromising her virtue.

Mel loved Ella as if she'd birthed her herself; especially growing up with a drug addict for a mother, she never truly bonded with her real mother. She felt a connection to Ella that Mel needed in her life. She always took what Ella said to heart, except when it came to her feelings for Connors and her love for him. Yes, she understood that he had a wife and soon a child at home; she'd known from day one but Mel unlike Ella truly believed that Connors loved her regardless of his situation at home.

"If he didn't Ma, why would he go through the trouble of putting money on my books every payday, sending money home to my momma and bringing me in all these nice things, knowing if he get caught he could lose his job? He risking it all for me Ma. Don't you see the band he bought me? Said it's our own lil promise ring;

promising that I'll be the only one he'll ever deal with, beside his wife of course and there ain't nothin' I can do about that. Look at it, ain't it beautiful," she said, flashing the sterling silver band with crushed diamonds inside.

To the average person it would've been considered a cheap pawn shop buy but to Mel it was as if he'd placed a ten carat rock on her finger. She didn't care where he got it from as long as it came from him.

"A married man can't promise you shit chil'! Shit but the fact that he goin' home every night; home to his wife! All that shit ain't nothin' more than hush money. Tid bits to keep you quiet so you don't go blabbin' yo' mouth and ruin what he really cares about, his home!"

"Ma there are so many women here that's willing to give it up to him for absolutely nothin' more than the fact that they can brag and say they gettin' some of his dick. He could've easily chose one of them, right? Right but he chose me and I don't ask him for anything, he just like to do things for me because we care about one another. Why is that so hard to believe," she asked Ella, thumbing through her locker for a can of Sprite.

"Cause you can't love another woman's husband lil girl, I keep telling you that. When are you gonna realize that God don't bless mess; especially mess you aware that you creating. It ain't right and can't nothin' good come of it. You just mark my words," Ella told her sitting on the bed and rolling her support stocking up her leg. "You coming to service?"

Mel leaned in and placed a kiss on Ella's cheek. She knew that she just wanted the best for her and was looking out for her.

"You know I'd go with you Ma but I don't know what's goin' on with me, I don't feel good. I think I ate somethin' that ain't

153

agreeing with me. I haven't been able to keep nothing down really and my tummy's been like hella tore up."

Ella looked at Mel as she parted her freshly curled grey hair and combed it over to the side.

"You ain't pregnant is you?"

Mel looked at Ella, taken aback by her question. *Pregnant?* The thought never crossed her mind. She chuckled at the thought. No way could she be pregnant.

"No I'm not pregnant Ma, why would you even say that," she asked, tickled by the insinuation.

"*Why would you even say that,*" Ella said, mimicking her.

Ella walked over to her, took the can of Sprite from her hand and stared at her.

"Ya'll use condoms every time ya'll have sex?" she asked, popping the top on the can and handing it back to her.

Mel almost dropped the can from her hand as she looked up at Ella. Ella could tell from the expression on her face that the answer was, no.

"Ever?"

Mel shook her head as she fumbled over her words.

"I... we... he... I ... we never... shit," she said, her head dropping down inside her hands. "What do I do if I am? No, I'm not tho, I would know if I was Ma. I'm not, trust me."

"Time ain't changed that damn much chil', is your period late?"

For as long as Mel could remember she had never had regular periods. They were always off from month-to-month so not seeing it at any given time wasn't cause for alarm to her. It's also the reason she never thought she could get pregnant.

Could I really be pregnant?

She sat back in the chair and looked up at Ella once again.

"I don't know Ma, it's always been funny actin' so I can't say with certainty but it can't be. God wouldn't play a sick joke on me like that would He?" she asked, watching as Ella applying her lipstick in the mirror.

"It's not God playing a sick joke on you, it's you playin' it on ya'self. Don't go blamin' the man upstairs for your stupidity downstairs. How could you not use a condom with this man, any man? You don't know what he does on the other side of that gate before and after he leaves here. You see he cheatin' on his wife with you, what makes you think you the only other one he's toyin' around' with?"

Mel thoughts drifted to Kieara and the night she caught them together. He had promised her however that he would never make that mistake again and Mel hadn't seen him near Kieara since. That spoke volumes to her. To Mel, it said that he respected her enough to keep his word and that he loved her. She truly couldn't bring herself to believe that he would have the need to be with anyone else besides her and his wife who was now limiting sex because of her furthering pregnancy.

"Ma I know you think it's wrong and maybe it is but it feels so right to me. I know he loves me and I'm his one and only. He loves me Ma, he does," she said, standing up and becoming light headed.

She reached for the top of Ella's locker to stabilize herself and Ella grabbed her arm and directed her over to her bed to lie down. She threw her crocheted purple and lilac blanket across Mel's legs. She grabbed a wash rag from her locker, went across the hall to wet it and dabbed Mel's forehead.

"Oh chil' you and yo' naivety reminds me of my Mary, so headstrong and stubborn; determined to do things yawls way when clearly God is tryin' to do it His way. It's aight to be stubborn but not when it's going against God's way. You'll lose every time baby, every time," she told Mel, handing her the can of Sprite again.

Mel sipped the soda and lay her head back on the pillow. She frowned at the overpowering smell of Ben gay that saturated the covers. She turned to face Ella.

"What if this is His way of doing things? I mean, all my life every since that day my cousin Brian had sex with me and put me to work for him, I been using my body to get what I want and what I need. I leaned that that was all people saw when they looked at me, my body, great sex and they were willing to pay me to get it.

Then when I went to work at the strip club I saw they were willing to pay me just to even watch me move that body. That's been my world Ma, that's all I've known. I never been on a date, I've never gotten flowers, I've never been dancing outside of that pole, and I've never done any of that mushy shit you see on TV.

It was always about money and business, until now. Yes I baited him in with my body but Ma, the things he says to me I've never heard before, not in truth. Niggah's would always say I had the best pus...coochie while they were up in it. Of course they'd say that at that moment," she paused as a tear rolled down the side of her face.

Ella took the towel and wiped it.

"I can't explain it Ma but his words are different, they sound different. They sound true. I feel something when he says them. And Ma, he doesn't just say them when we're having sex. He tells me in the cards he sends when he send me money, he tells me in passing or after he just kissed me for no reason at all."

"Lust is always more exciting than love, you remember that. And this is not God's doing cause God don't specialize in breaking His own Commandments. I can understand what you feel Mel, I can. Hell I was young once but you gotta know that nothin' good can come of this because it's wrong, you hear me Mel, it's wrong!

Somewhere out there is a woman that trusts that when her husband, her husband Mel, leaves out the front door to go to work every day; that he's going to make a living for her and their family, not make whoopee with some other woman.

Now you've had it rough, I know but baby God has something better in store for you. A man someday that will give you all the feelings this man gave you and more. Except this one will belong to you, nobody but you. But you gotta be in order to get it. He can't bless you while you outta order baby girl, He just can't.

Now I'm going to service. You welcome to lay here until you get yo' legs back underneath you. I'll see about Mae getting us into sick call in morning for a pregnancy test."

Mel's eyes widened as she grabbed Ella's arm and shook her head.

"We can't, I won't…."

"We can and you will. What you think you 'pose to do, lay around with a possible baby growing inside you unattended to? You know you have to find out one way or another. Don't worry Mae been my friends over eleven years, she'll be discreet," she told Mel, rising up from the bed.

Ella grabbed her Bible and headed out the room. Mel lay there, looking up at the squared cork board Ella had above her bed; rows and rows of pictures of her family; from her sons doing prison time in scattered facilities to her great grandchildren she had yet to have the opportunity to see.

Kids? Me?

She had cared for her brother and sisters coming up but Mel had never envisioned herself as a mother. Could the Heavens have smiled down on her and blessed her with a child from the only man she'd ever loved?

Mel shrugged her shoulders and discarded the thought. She just didn't see the possibility of her being pregnant but as she rolled over, reached out for the green trash can nearby and watched the clear liquid expel itself from her body; she began to have her doubts. *It's gotta be just a virus or something, right,* she tried to convince herself.

Connors was off the next two nights so she needed to focus on getting better before he returned. From the card he'd sent her the day before with her bi-weekly allowance, there were many things he had in store for her upon his return to duty. They had developed a code language to keep the mail room clerk at bay.

I can't wait till I come visit you again (Come to work). Better yet I can't wait for you to get home. There is so many things I wanna do to you. Fuckin' you in the grass (on the pool table in the Rec room), bending you over the Jacuzzi (the toilet), maybe the kitchen counter (his desk), or maybe I'll just stand you up in the foyer amongst the coats and jackets (closest) and dominate that pussy!

Missing you! See you s⊙⊙n!

The "*O*'s" in soon was always two fish beside each other, his zodiac sign of Pieces. She couldn't wait to see him, smell him, and feel him so she needed to conquer this cold and quick. But as she stared down at the white piece of paper Mae had brought to Ella the following day, Mel finally realized that it would be a long time before she would be able to kick what she'd contracted.

UCG, Positive.

Mel and Ella had gotten up early, gone to sick call and Mae was able to slip the small clear cup to Ella for Mel to fill. Mel filled it with confidence that it would return negative but as she sat on the bed, tears running down her face, she now had to face the fact that her life, Connors life and everyone else it affected was about to change… in which direction, she had no idea.

Charlene and Nikki had been awake since four am count. Nikki had washed and flat ironed Charlene's hair and she looked astonishing. She couldn't dress in street clothes until she got over to Receiving & Discharge. The goodbye party her friends had given her was one she would always remember. She loved them but she couldn't lie, she was so ready to walk out that release gate and go claim what was rightfully hers… Marco, her kids and the family they had built together.

Charlene began to pack up the things she wanted to ship home. She only took the things she knew she would hold on to, things that mattered. Nikki's blanket would go on the bus with her, pictures she'd taken over the years with her kids, Marco and her mom as well as those she'd taken with her friends on the compound. Everything else such as letters from home, artwork from her kids and certificates from classes she'd taken, she packed away. Things such as food, clothes, hygiene products and craft items she left behind for less fortunate inmates. Charlene knew that Nikki would make sure someone who would truly appreciated them would receive them.

Charlene looked down at the diamond encrusted cross on her necklace and then over to Nikki who was staring off at the wall. She removed the chain from around her neck and walked over to her friend.

"I want you to have this and I want you to never take if off."

"Lena, I can't…"

"You can and you will. Promise you'll never take it off," she said, latching the chain behind Nikki's neck.

160

"You know I promise. I love you Lena. From the first day I saw you hit the comp, I noticed you were different. Some people blend right in here and some you just can't imagine what curve life could have thrown at them to land them in a place like this. You have always set apart from a lot of these miserable bitches in here and that's what drew me too you. Don't you ever, ever come back here. You don't belong here, remember that."

They hugged and they both let go of the emotions they had been holding in. Both were afraid for different reasons… Charlene hadn't been home in years. Nikki was afraid she wouldn't be the same once her friend left; that she wouldn't want to let anyone else close to her because she was tired of watching people she loved walk away from her.

"You ready to do this?" Nikki asked her, wiping her eyes. "You ready to nail that muthafucka to the wall?"

"Ready to hang 'em like a picture baby," Charlene said, taking the tiny plastic bag from the cooler and drying it off with her washcloth.

She tucked the bag down between her ass cheeks. Time had come for her to go downstairs and wait for the shuttle van. On the way downstairs she stopped and give hugs to all the women she'd come to care about. Once downstairs, Nikki had once again gave her instructions on what to do.

"As soon as you get to the counter Lena, you hear me?"

"I hear you. I'll call your phone tonight after count okay? Have it on," she said, beginning to cry again.

Her stomach began to turn into knots as the white shuttle van pulled up in front of the building. Nikki, Tae and the rest of Charlene's friends stood on the porch watching as Charlene walked her way to freedom. Nikki called after her and when

161

Charlene turned around, Nikki began clapping her hand and playing patty cake with Charlene from a distance, mimicking the Color Purple.

"You and me will never part."

Everyone started laughing and Charlene and Nikki simultaneously burst out into tears as she boarded the shuttle. Tae pulled Nikki in her arms as Bright Eyes sucked her teeth behind them. Nikki lay her head in Tae's chest and let it go.

"Come on lil momma, you knew this day would come right? You wanted this for her right?"

Nikki shook her head in Tae's chest. Yes she wanted it for her friend more than anything; to return to a normal life of being a mother, daughter and hopefully a wife one day... not inmate #81916-022.

"You still got me baby."

Bright Eyes brushed past Tae and bumped them on her way back inside the camp. As always Tae got Nikki to smile.

"You know yo' bitch crazy right?" she asked, wiping her face. "Somethin' is really wrong with that hoe."

"That hoe ain't mine, not no mo'." Tae sighed; relieved she was finally rid of Bright Eyes and the silly games she played.

Charlene looked back, waved at Nikki and Tae for as long as she could see them through the small square window in the back of the van. Tears were rolling down her face as the van pulled into the gates of the adjacent men's FMC.

Her stomach was queasy as she thought really hard about abandoning the plan she and Nikki had put together. After all, it was over now right?

I made it out, I survived it. Does it really matter now?

Yes it did, according to Nikki.

"You gotta do it for the next one Lena who may not be as strong as you are to make it through. He's gotta pay for the sick shit he's done to you," Nikki told her.

Charlene was handed her cardboard box with her clothes from the discharge officer and as she dressed, all she could think about was Marco and the kids. How seeing them and laying next to them would soon be a reality.

Charlene walked into the changing room; undressed and removed the small bag nestled between her cheeks and placed it on the wooden bench beside her. She removed the clothes from the box her mom had sent and began dressing. She looked over herself in the mirror. Marco had paid for her coming home outfit, a pair of curve fitting Miss Me jeans, a pair of Coach crème colored sandals, a crème colored see through Miss Me t-shirt with diamond studs, a white tank for underneath and a crème and brown Coach purse. He had always done such a wonderful job picking out things for her.

"My man still know my taste," she smiled, running her hands around her ass. She tossed the prison issued scrubs in the bin across the room and exhaled a deep sigh. It would be the last time she would feel them against her skin.

She picked up the tiny bag and tucked it inside her hand. When she walked back out and reached the discharge desk, the officer gave her a stack of papers to look over and sign. A bus ticket and sixty dollars to eat on her way back to Ohio. Charlene knew that it was now or never as she rubbed the bag inside her palm with her fingers.

"I... I... I need to see the Warden Hayes. I have something very important to talk to him about and I mean so important, he should come running."

"Is that right? That important huh? Well why don't you tell me and let me be the judge of just how important it is," the female guard told her, putting a paper clip on Charlene's paper work and setting it to the side.

"I'd rather tell the Warden."

Charlene wanted to curse the short chubby woman out but she had to remember that until she got onto the other side of that metal fence, she was still in custody.

"Well the Warden is busy right now so whatever it is will just have to wait. You probably can have yo' PO call him or your caseworker call him when you reach the halfway house. Now your bus leaves in 3 hours so you gone endure a wait at the station but the shuttle is waiting for you."

Charlene grabbed the items from the counter top and looked at the officer one last time before she began to walk off. She was so glad she wouldn't have to see any of them again. They were just so sickening to her.

She took a few steps but turned back and leaned into the counter.

"No, I don't think I'll wait Officer Simmons," she said looking at her name tag. "And when the Feds ask me why I didn't report that I had been repeatedly sexually assaulted while being held at one of their facilities, I'll make sure I let them know that I tried but Officer Simmons said the Warden was too busy to listen. What do

164

you think they will say? Especially when I'm holding his semen in the palm of my hand!"

Officer Simmons took a step back, bewildered at not only what she had heard the tiny bag Charlene had just placed on her counter.

"Are you serious?"

"Do I look serious?" Charlene asker her. "Would you like for me to open it so you can see for yourself?"

Officer Simmons immediately radioed for Deputy Warden Hayes to come down to R&D. For the next forty-five minutes, Warden and his staff listened as Charlene told them the gruesome details of Tucker's behavior towards her and other inmates.

When asked for the sperm sample. Charlene refused to turn it over to anyone associated with the prison. She demanded they call in the FBI. Then and only then would she give up the only proof she had, not after everything she had gone through.

She could hear Nikki's voice in her ear.

"You better get 'em bitch!"

Charlene chuckled to herself and forty minutes later, a Federal agent bagged and tagged the specimen as the other taped her statement. When she was done the Feds offered to escort her to the bus station themselves so they could continue to talk to her along the way.

When they left her at the Greyhound station on NW New Circle Road, they told her that they would be in contact with her through her PO within a few days.

Charlene felt so relieved it was over for the most part and she was so proud of herself for sticking up for herself. It would've been so easy to just keep quiet and let it go but she was glad she stood her ground even if just for the others as Nikki pointed out.

Her first taste of freedom, she walked into the bus station and over to the counter. She gave the attendant the ticket, checked in and decided to grab a bite to eat before boarding the bus. It had been so long since she'd had fast food but on her way to Burger King, she saw the pay phones and decided she needed to call and inform Marco of the time her bus was scheduled to arrive at the station.

She had tried to call him the night before from Nikki's cell phone but the phone kept going to voicemail. She bought a Whopper meal to get some change for the pay phone. After she stuffed down the flamed broiled burger and fries, she called Marco's phone and it felt funny to hear the phone answered without the prison recording playing, asking them if they would accept the call. What wasn't funny, was hearing Tiffany's voice come through the receiver.

"Where's Marco?"

"Who may I tell him is calling?"

"You know damn well who this is, it's Charlene. I'm so sure he told you I was coming home today?"

"You know what, you're right. I think he did mention something about that to me last night. Well welcome home, did you like the outfit I picked out for you?"

"You picked out? Where the fuck is Marco?" Charlene snapped.

Why is this bitch still there? If Marco told her I was coming home why ain't this bitch gone? And why is he letting his hoe pick out my clothes?

"What's up Lena?"

166

"What's up Lena? No what's up Marco? What the hell is going on? Why is she still at my house and why is she telling me she picked out my outfit?"

"Lena, she still here… cause she lives here."

Charlene felt the earth move underneath her and her heart drop down inside her stomach. He couldn't have said what she thought he'd said. Live there?

"What?" she whispered. "Since when?"

"For the last year. I ain't wanna tell you while…"

"The last year? You mean the last year we been talking, writing and fucking? Making plans to be together and all along you had a bitch living in my house? You playing games Marco? How the fuck could you do that to me, Marco?"

"Lena calm down. I ain't wanna tell you while you was in there and have you buggin' out. Now you finna hit the bricks, you can get on with your life. Look I'll always love you Lena, you the mother of my kids but I'm doin' somethin' different now… with Tiff."

"With Tiffany? With Tiffany? Marco I sat all these years in jail for you, remember that? I took this case because I loved you and I ain't wanna see you away from us for life and this is how you repay me? You play me? And then say fuck me, you moving on? I can't believe you… no… no... I won't let you do this Marco!" she screamed into the receiver. "You hear me Marco? That is my family, not hers, mine!"

The operator came on the line and told Charlene she had fifteen seconds remaining. She dug in her pockets for more change but couldn't find any.

"Wait... wait Marco... baby wait... don't do this to me... I'm comin' home baby, I'm comin' home. To my family... to our family," she cried.

"Not anymore Lena. Now I gotta go, I gotta go to work. Your mom has the kids so they'll be with her when she meets you at the bus station."

With that he hung up the phone. Charlene stood there and stared at the receiver, tears beginning to fall from her eyes. Everything she had been looking forward to was now gone. The last year had been nothing but one big lie. Marco had done exactly what Nikki had said, he made sure he was the first to get between her legs and had done it with deception and ill intentions.

Charlene's tears fell harder as she thought back over everything she'd endured from start to finish for the sake of him and their children. She felt like a fool. Her inside threatened to turn up-side-down.

She gathered her things, walked outside, handed the driver her ticket and boarded the bus, headed for the unknown. What would she do now? She sat down in the black and burgundy striped seat, placed her box in the seat beside her, opened it up and retrieved the blanket Nikki had given her. She leaned back in the seat, covered herself with the warmth of a friends love and cried.

Chapter Twenty

Tae had spent the last twenty-four hours dealing with Bright Eyes' up and down emotions; from breakfast notes of death threats to those and hour later pleading for them to talk. It wasn't the first time Tae had dealt with the insanity of a woman scorned but it was the first time she was trapped inside the same perimeters.

It seemed that everywhere she turned, she ran into Bright Eyes; breakfast, the hallway, the bathroom, lunch and dinner. After breakfast as she stood on the porch of the camp holding Nikki as they said goodbye to their home girl Charlene, Bright Eyes made it clear she didn't like what she saw. She stormed by bumping up hard against Tae's shoulder using her pointed elbow to poke Tae in the chest.

She heard Nikki's smart comment about her being a crazy hoe but she paid that no mind. What pissed her off was Tae's response, that she was no longer her headache. Bright Eyes stormed up to her room, grabbed her yellow writing pad and began scribbling.

I fuckin' hate you! How could you do this to me? You so busy tryin' to stunt fo' these lousy hoes that you forget who has really been holdin' you down all this time. How could you make me love you when you knew damn well you had no plans of lovin' me back? All you wanna do is run around with these nothin' ass bitches in yo' face... do you Boo! Fuck you and them nasty ass hoes! Hope you swallow somethin' and yo' throat swell and die bitch!

Tae just shook her head and laughed. Bright Eyes was still so young and she had no clue how to handle life yet. She had no understanding of how her own actions had brought about the demise of their situation. Tae was done, plain and simple. She wasn't denying that she cared for Bright Eyes because truth be told; she cared, maybe even more than she wanted too. She knew that Bright Eyes didn't really have anyone on the outside and that was one of the reasons she acted the way she did but Tae also knew she couldn't trust the imbalance of Bright Eyes' on edge personality.

It's one thing to be on guard from those you know are out to get you but to be on guard with the one you're lying with was just insane. After what she'd done to Shawna, Tae felt that she simply couldn't trust Bright Eyes anymore and that she could not handle.

Bright Eyes would be leaving soon so Tae, while definitive in the stands that she would never deal with her on that level again, did feel that after things calmed down a bit, she would sit down with Bright Eye's and be open to them retaining some type of friendship. She wasn't a cold hearted woman by far and she did realize how Bright Eyes had stepped up when she needed her too. Yet in any kind of hustle game, trust outweighed any other quality you could possess and Tae had none left for her.

Besides, that day Tae's focus had been solely on Nikki and the loss of their friend. Tae had held her as she cried that morning and she knew this would be a difficult time for her. Nikki and Charlene were as close as two people could be and being locked down made losing someone all the more difficult. They'd eaten lunch together under the watchful eyes of Bright Eyes.

"You know she stalkin' us right?" Nikki joked.

"She ain't a bad person but she only been in one relationship in her life; the niggah she on her case with. He gone fo' life, her family ain't really fuckin' with her so she just kinda tryin' to find her way. Mentally, she still a baby. I ain't sayin' give her a pass on shit; I'm just sayin' I understand her. It ain't the silly shit she do I'm holdin' against her, it's the major shit. I do too much dirt to be with a muthafucka that can turn on me cause shit ain't going' her way, feel me?"

"Hell yeah I feel you. That's why you see me fuck with only a few of these chicks. My patience is like zero tolerance for the dumb shit. It's kinda cool that you recognize the fact that she got issues but that's exactly why you shoulda known she was gon' be one of them possessive psycho hoes. I've learn the hard way that when these chicks have no outside life, they tend to be overly clingy to the one on the inside."

"You learned huh?" Tae teased. "You mean you gave somebody that pussy and I been beggin' fo it all this damn time?"

"Whatever niggah, you so full of shit. You was caught up wit' yo' girl over there and I don't have time to have to whoop one of these lil clucks' ass over no bullshit. And that one," she said, pointing to Bright Eyes. "Would be a prime candidate. I'm sayin' tho, what the fuck you do to her? She runnin' round here like a fiend searchin' for a crumb of crack on the floor," Nikki joked.

"Why don't you stop fronting, asking all these round-the-way questions and find out for yo 'self what I can do. Clearly by yo' own admission you been down this road before. Damn bitch I ain't askin' fo' your hand in marriage, just some pussy."

Nikki laughed and shook her head. Besides Charlene, Tae was the closest to her. She had other women she dealt with at a distance but she was much closer, much more personal with Tae and Charlene. They thought alike, they liked the same things, they got along in a way that both knew that even outside the confinement of prison, they would have definitely still been friends.

As they all assembled for mail call that evening, Tae and Nikki sat down in the lobby across from the officer's station door, leaning up against the off white colored wall. Once again the hawking eyes of Tae's ex was singed upon them.

"I ought to fuck you just to give her a reason to keep looking at me sideways," Nikki laughed. "Aye least she'd actually have a reason not to like me."

"I don't give a fuck why you do it, dammit just do it!"

"Shut the fuck up, you will not have me all up in here lookin' crazy next to that helfa. You will not be adding me to your trophy case bitch."

As she and Tae play fought with one another, Officer Tucker began placing the piles of mail on top of the red door ledge. Before he could begin calling name however, a group of roughly ten officers ran up inside the camp's front door and told the inmates to clear the floor, stand up and back up against the wall. The only time they saw this maneuver was right before a massive compound shake down where a security team came in, made all the women exit the building and brought in the drug dogs, searching every square inch of the property

Nikki looked at Tae.

"Bitch is you dirty?"

Tae in turn looked to Bright Eyes who hadn't had a hand in this one but knew that if this was a shakedown, Tae had enough contraband in her room to send her away to county and most certainly and FCI. In her own sad way, Bright Eyes wouldn't have minded at all; figuring that she loved Tae so much that if she couldn't have her, she damn sure didn't want to watch her everyday with someone else.

"Like a pig in slop," Tae responded.

"You don't think she," Nikki paused, putting her hand over her mouth. "That bitch wouldn't?"

"Shittt, I don't put nothin' past no muthafucka right about now. Hell hath no fury…"

"Like a bitch scorned," Nikki chimed in, sucking her teeth.

They watched as the guards directed the women to the wall space around the area. To their surprise, the lettering on the back of the jackets they wore said FBI and when two of the agents drew down their guns on Tucker everybody looked at the spectacle in shock. Everybody except Nikki of course who hit Tae on the arm and smiled to herself; realizing that Charlene had gone through with their plan. The agent in charge told Tucker he was being arrested and Nikki burst out laughing.

"Russell Tucker, you are under arrest for violating US Statue §1896.5 Rape in the 2nd Degree and US Statue §7609.1 Sexual Assault in the 1st Degree. You have the right to remain silent, anything you say…"

"Gone Lena! That bitch did it! She fuckin' did it!" Nikki said, balling Tae's shirt up in her fists and pulling on her arm. "O-m-g, we partying tonight bitch fuck that! We celebrating! My girl got that dirty dick muthafucka!"

Bright Eyes looked at Nikki and wondered why she was so excited to witness the scene unfolding in front of their eyes. But more so than that, she watched Tae's reaction to Nikki and it bothered her to see something in Tae's eyes she hadn't seen since the first day they arrived on the compound together… want.

I have to do something, something to keep this from happening, Bright Eyes told herself. She needed to get Tae alone, somewhere where she could tell her how she felt; apologize to her and make her understand why she had done what she had done. Make her see that it was all for them, a stronger them. All she needed was an opportunity to remind Tae why she'd been the chosen one in Tae's life up until that point.

After dinner, Tae came into her room to grab a Black & Mild from inside her locker when she noticed a card on top, next to all the things that become her favorite prison meals… clam and chicken fried rice, burritos, chicken salad and lemon cheese cake from scratch. Tae picked up the card.

A truce maybe? I just wanna start by saying I'm so very sorry for all I've done. In my own way I thought I was doin' what was right. Yes, some of it was for my own personal gain but I also thought that if I got rid of her, you could completely take over the game in here and come up. I know that's not an excuse but it's true.

You've been my heart since day one we hit this compound and I love you so much with all my heart. I am hoping that you can remember why you loved me so much and not just the bad things I've done. I miss you, I miss your kiss and I miss your touch. I know you need some time but can we please talk soon.

I noticed you didn't eat at dinner... I know you hate meatloaf, so I made you your favs... hope it warms your tummy and ur heart.

Luv

Bright Eyes

The card had caught Tae off guard and she had to admit, she liked the gesture. She thought about talking to her, explaining why she felt they couldn't be together on that level again which would hopefully make things a little easier for Bright Eyes to deal with. Tae unlike any other woman on that compound knew the softer side of Bright Eyes, the one that just wanted to be loved and cared about.

Instead though she decided to simply slip a return note under her pillow thanking her for the food and card. She told her that they would indeed talk soon.

174

Tae grabbed her Black & Mild, the food from the lock top and headed down the stairs. Nikki was waiting for her under the pavilion with a joint and some E&J Brandy hidden in an empty Coke can.

"I see you ain't learned yet, I told you that chick gone have you round here with one finger, no thumbs and bald headed with no clit," Nikki told Tae, laughing and handing her the can of Coke.

"Well fuck it, if she do knock me; let me get some of that fire before I go!"

"Asshole," Nikki said, rolling her eyes as Tae sat down behind her, legs gaped open on each side of her. "I wonder what Lena is doing right now; I miss her ass so much already."

Tae heard the sadness in Nikki's voice and it hurt her to see Nikki who was for the most part, always such an upbeat person hurting the way she was. Tae put the white plastic fork down inside the clear plastic bowl of rice and scooted up the wooden bench closer to Nikki. She moved Nikki's hair from her face and brushed it with her fingers to the back of her neck. She placed her arms around Nikki's waist from behind and squeezed her.

"Ain't no tellin' what she into, probably just gettin' settled into the halfway house. Don't trip; you know she'll be callin' you soon. I know allot of people fake it til' they make out to them streets but not ya'll. What ya'll share is tru and its real. Anybody could see that and that's why allot of these clucks around here don't like ya'll cause they wish they had it too. Now I thought we was celebrating," she asked Nikki, placing a soft kiss on the blade of her shoulder.

Nikki turned her head to the side and laid back against Tae's shoulder, secretly loving the feel of Tae's lips on her neck and shoulder. Tae took her headphones from around her neck and picked up the empty white Styrofoam cup sitting on the table. She stuck her thumbs through the bottom creating a hole and then took the fork, laid the cup on its side and poked holes in the cup. She placed an earphone on each end of the cup thus making a portable speaker. As Floetry came flowing through the handmade speaker, Tae fired up the Black & Mild and snuggled close to Nikki under the light of the moon. She could feel Nikki's body shaking, she was crying for her friend. Tae took her finger and wiped Nikki's tears as the music, liquor and stimulant took them to a mellow mental space.

"...see I been watchin' you for awhile, your smile and I don't know if I can be with you for the night, aight? Is that aight baby..."

Tae took her white face towel from inside the waistband of her light grey sweats and wiped Nikki's face again.

"She miss you just as much, you know that right? Come mere," she told her, telling Nikki to stand up, turn around and sit down facing her.

Tae pulled her close, placing each one of her legs across each of her thighs. She held her tightly against her body, kissing her tears from her cheeks.

"... we could take the step to see, if this is really gonna be, all you gotta do is say yes..."

Nikki looked at Tae and she didn't know if it was the circumstances surrounding the moment, the liquor or what but at that moment she was feeling Tae in a way she couldn't explain but she didn't care. She caught Tae by surprise as she grabbed the front of Tae's wife beater and snatched her to her lips; the salt of her tears mixing with the taste of liquor on their tongues.

Tae had waited for this moment for so long but deep inside, so had Nikki and all the passion they had pent up inside came spilling over inside that kiss.

176

"... all you gotta do is say yes, don't deny what you feel, let me undress you baby. Open up your mind and just rest, I'm about to let you know that you make me so, so, so, so, so, so, so, so..."

Tae put her hand underneath Nikki's shirt and squeezed her small B cup sized breasts. Nikki squirmed up against Tae's body and told her that her touch felt so good.

"What is it about you that make muthafucka's go crazy? Is it this touch?" Nikki asked her as she gyrated against Tae. "Show me Tae, show me what the fuck it is."

Tae took her hand and pulled Nikki's dark grey shorts and panties to the side and slid her finger inside Nikki's very tight but wet mommy. A new inmate who had arrived a few weeks ago came outside and took a seat at the wooden picnic table directly behind them to smoke a cigarette.

Tae was about to remove her fingers but Nikki grabbed her hand and told her not to stop.

"Fuck her, don't stop... fuck me."

That turned Tae on beyond measure as she thrust her fingers inside a moaning Nikki's mommy while the inmate pretended to look off in the opposite direction. The moonlight, the music, Tae's touch plus the fact that she knew the inmate was watching sent Nikki over the edge as Tae felt the muscles in Nikki's mommy began to pulsate against her fingers.

Nikki grabbed the back of Tae's shirt and she dug her nails in her back. She bit down on Tae's shoulder and Tae moaned in ecstasy as Nikki's body slowly recovered. The inmate got up from the table, flicked her cigarette butt on the ground and began walking towards the building.

"Its count time," she spat out, sounding annoyed.

Tae and Nikki burst out laughing.

"You mad bitch?" Nikki yelled after her.

"You somethin' else you know that? Why you do that to that girl?" Tae asked her.

"Why you let me, you coulda stopped."

When the inmate reached her room for count, she looked up to Bright Eyes. She was a little thrown by what she had just witnessed. She could have sworn she had seen that same woman exiting the shower with her Bunkie a week or so before. So in high style prison drama fashion, she asked Bright Eyes about it.

"Did you use to date the cute stud; ya know the one with the braids?"

"Yeah why, still do, we just into it right now." Bright Eyes questioned her, jumping down off her bunk for count. "What about her?"

"Well I ain't messy or nothin' but damn, these chicks move quick. I just seen her outside under the pavilion with a chick and they weren't just talkin'," she said, in true messy fashion.

"So what were they doin'?"

"Probably the same thing you and her was doing in that shower a week ago."

Bright Eyes looked spitefully at the young white inmate and began biting down on her tongue. Nikki, she cringed to herself. No wonder she couldn't meet me tonight to talk, the bitch out there freakin' with that bitch! All good, I got something fo' this hoe!

178

She spent standing count coming up with a plan to teach Tae the lesson of a lifetime. Getting shipped away, her or Nikki wouldn't be enough, she determined as she turned to wipe her face away from the other women. No, the pain she felt at that moment she desperately wanted to inflict upon Tae... that and then some.

She waited for about fifteen minutes after count when she knew that like clockwork, Tae would be in the phone room downstairs waiting to call her beloved Kelly. Once she knew the coast was clear, Bright Eyes hurried down to her room in her white robe and shower shoes, walked past the doorway and quickly looked inside to make sure Meko was gone as well. She knew that Tae couldn't order a new lock for a few more days at commissary so she dipped inside, turned the lock, popped it open and took the missing piece she needed to set her plan in motion.

Bright Eyes returned the lock, crept back down the hall to her room, climbed on her bunk and smiled to herself. Young or not, Tae had underestimated her and for that mistake, she was about to pay... dearly.

Mel had spent the last 48 hours thinking of all the what if's...
*What if he get angry? What if he leaves his wife for me? What if
he never wants to see me again? What if they find out and ship me
off? OMG what if he gets fired because of me?*

Mel couldn't have prepared herself however for the reaction she
got as she sat across the desk from him in his office the following
night. Mel had hesitated to tell him, so afraid of how he'd react but
as she heard Ella's voice in her ear she knew it had to be done and
so she began to utter the words to him softly and slowly.

*"Since you're so sure he wants to be with you, tell him and see his
response. He loves you right? That's what you keep sayin' and you
seem so sure of it right? Well if he truly loves you like you hoping
he do, he'll do the right thing and do right by you. He'll do
whatever he has to do to make it right for you."*

"I'm sorry," Mel told him, taking the responsibility or lack thereof,
on her shoulders and off of his. "I should have been more
responsible. I get everything else snuck onto this compound, I
could've gotten a box of condoms," she told him, feeling her
emotions beginning to build up inside her.

Mel looked up at Connors who had come around the desk, walked
over to the doorway and made sure it was clear before closing the
door. He walked back over to the grey chair next to Mel and sat
down. He picked up her hand inside of his and with the other he
raised her head to him.

"Are you sure? Are you absolutely sure?"

Mel shook her head as she felt the tears fall from her eyes. She
wasn't crying at the results of the tests, she was hurt because she

knew that she was the cause of a life altering event in the life of the man she loved more than life.

"I'm sorry," she broke down. "I didn't try too; I promise I didn't try to. I don't blame you if you never want to see me again but please believe me, I didn't try to fuck up your life or your home. Please, you gotta believe me," she sobbed in his chest.

He raised her head once again to him and Mel's heart began to break as she saw a tear roll down his face.

"Shhhhhh, quiet down now. Stop it baby, stop it, ok? This wasn't on you, this was on me. You didn't hold a gun to my head and make me drop my boxers. I knew what I was doing. I *knew* better than to do this with you but it's what I wanted to do. I knew the risks I was taking. No I didn't see this coming but I chose to play the game and this was the outcome. An extreme one but the outcome none the less and it's on me. *I'm* the married one, *me* not you. It's my job to protect home, not *yours*.

You're in here, there's no way your mind should be on sneaking in condoms when I coulda easily stopped at the fuckin' gas station on my way to work," he said kissing her on the lips. "It's not like I didn't know that every time I laid eyes on you, I had to touch you."

"Maybe but I bet you regret the day you started fuckin' with me huh?" she asked turning her face from him.

Connors didn't like to see her like this. He was use to seeing her so perky, confident and bold. He saw the broken insecure little girl sitting in front of him and it hurt him that he had a hand in making her feel this way. He pulled her face back to his.

"Never, I never would nor could. I love you Melody. Baby you have touched my life in ways I never thought was possible. You've brought me happiness, satisfaction, passion, intensity, entertainment... you brought me life, life Melody. How could I regret that? Our paths would've never crossed in life outside of here and I'm so glad they did.

No I don't regret one moment I've spent with you but I'll admit, I'm not overjoyed at the outcome. Even under different circumstances with you being on the outside baby I'd still be married and this," he said, placing a hand on her stomach. "As much as I wish it could, still couldn't happen."

He wiped her eyes with his thumbs. It wasn't quite the words Mel wanted to hear. *Yes* he had reassured her that he indeed cared both about her and their relationship but he had also made it known that he cared about home above all.

Mel had hoped that he'd in some way figure out a way for her to keep their unborn child. After all in her mind it was the link that could tie them together forever. She even went so far as to suggest she lie and tell the Camp Administrator that she'd snuck off the compound with an ex-boyfriend, had gone to a hotel and had gotten herself pregnant.

It certainly wasn't unheard of for women to leave the grounds; inside the trunks or ducked down behind the seats of cars down at the bottom of the hill to go to hotels, bars, etc. and in Mel's twisted fantasy, she thought that somehow admitting she'd broken the rules, would allow her to hold onto the love child they'd created together.

Her plan was simple. She would probably be transferred to an FCI for breaking the camp rules but as long as he wrote to her and sent her a little money to make sure she was okay, she could hold their secret close to her heart and nurture their child now growing inside her.

She would demand nothing of him concerning his home life nor his wife. She understood that they came first regardless of who or what. All she wanted was to bear his child and upon release be his home away from home. Mel truly didn't care if she was second, she was willing to be that as long as it took, even if that meant forever.

Now here he was, explaining to her that the bond they shared in DNA form would have to be terminated; that he could never risk his wife finding out about his act of betrayal to their vows, especially not at this level.

"Melody baby, I can't let you have this baby. There's just no way you can. Do you truly understand how this jeopardizes my life? How this could end my career and land me behind bars? They don't tolerate this kind of thing Melody. You haven't thought this through. You can't have a baby," he said standing up from the chair.

He began to pace back and forth and Mel felt bad that she had upset him.

"Think about it. You're in prison, who is gonna come and get the baby from the hospital, your mother because you know I can't. Who is gonna care for it until you get home and mind you, if you tell them you've been off the compound baby you may end up with even more time. You definitely gone lose any good time you earned, you know that."

Mel knew that what he was saying was true and that trying to have his child would do both of them more harm than it could do good. She knew her mother couldn't care for a small child, she was struggling enough with the siblings she already had to care for.

Connors was right, she hadn't thought of the true legal ramifications to her sentence if she admitted she'd broken the camp rules to that extreme. Even though what he said made sense to her, it didn't make the reality hurt any less and Connors knew that as he pulled her up from the chair and held her close. Mel lay her head on his shoulder and inhaled his pacifying scent. It calmed her along with the soothing feel of his arms around her. He placed a series of soft kisses on her shoulders and neck as he whispered in her ear.

"I wish it didn't have to be like this baby, I truly do. In another time, before our lives took the turn they did, I would be so happy with you, I know that."

Mel pulled her head back and looked him in the eyes.

"You would?"

Connors didn't answer; he just leaned in, kissed her lips with slow deliberate kisses that touched her soul. Mel felt saddened that the reality that Ella had constantly drilled into her head was coming to be.

A man will never leave his home for you and even if he does, it's only temporary. He will go back, they always do. And if he does, why would you want him? He left her, he'd leave you too.

Mel shook her head at the thought. Why *couldn't it be another lifetime*, She questioned. *Why couldn't I have crossed paths with him in St. Louis?*

Connors rubbed her back and told her everything would be okay. That he would figure it all out and that no matter what, he would always love her. Mel fell into his words and his touch, knowing that his rotation was coming to an end the following week and that if he in fact arranged an abortion for her, that this could very well be the last night that had to share together, she had to have him.

"Tell me again. Please just say it again," she pleaded, kissing him on the cheeks.

"I love you," he whispered. "I'll always love you Melody."

He slid his hands down her back to her ass and gripped it. He pulled her body close to his.

"I've never felt anything in my life like what I feel for you. All my life, every since I was a little girl men have looked at me like I had nothing more to offer the world but my body. Nobody Cared about who I really was on the inside and well... I guess I'm to blame for that one as well. I never really thought I had much to offer myself."

Connors put his finger to her lips.

"Shhh... that's bullshit and I never want to hear you say it again. Yes, your body is a beautiful work of art and a man would be lying to himself if he said he wasn't dying to touch it, see it or feel it or at least thinking about it. But Melody you have a lot more to offer than that.

Look at how you are around here. Always going out of way to help someone in need, giving them food, your clothes, doing their hair... you are such a giving person and you never ask for anything in return. Your heart is beautiful and..."

Mel rushed his mouth, his braces pinching the inside of her lips she pressed against them so hard. She put her heart into the intensity of her kiss. All the emotions she'd felt over the last 48 hours came pouring out into her lips.

She loved him, he loved her... both with a forbidden love that both knew could go no further but one that neither wanted to be without.

Connors put his hands underneath her shirt and unlatched her bra. He massaged her breasts as Mel fell completely into his touch. She gripped his shirt as their tongues danced. He began to kiss all over her face.

"Tonight I don't wanna fuck you; I wanna make love to you, from head to toe. I want you to know how I feel about you. Meet me in the fitness room in half an hour. Let me do my rounds real quick."

Connors lay three blue exercise mats down onto the speckled tile of the fitness room floor and latched them together via the black Velcro. He had grabbed a blanket from one of the empty rooms along his rounds and he lay it across the mats.

He told Mel to lie down as he grabbed another mat, walked to the door and placed it over the small square window. He walked back over to her lying naked below him on the blanket, looking up at him and he smiled.

Connors looked at his watch. He had two hours before count time. He stood over her, never breaking eye contact as he undressed in front of her. Mel's nipples hardened, her mommy moistened as she waited to see his entire naked body for the first time. She took in every inch of him; his hardened chocolate chest, his ripped arms, thin waist, strong thighs and his solid jimmy upward at attention.

Mel moaned at the sight before her and Connors jimmy responded with a slight jerk. This would be the first time their fully naked bodies touched one another and as he kneeled down on the mat between her legs, the anticipation made Mel's mommy throb.

Connors however, planned to do exactly what he'd told her, kiss her body from head to toe. He towered above her, briefly staring her in the eyes before leaning down to kiss her on the forehead. Mel loved his kisses because he always parted his lips, letting the moist tip of his tongue seep through his lips with each kiss.

She closed her eyes and placed her hands on his chest as he kissed her from cheek-to-cheek, eye-to-eye, the bridge of her noise, the rim of her mouth, her neck, her shoulder blades, her arms and stomach. He ran his tongue between her fingers before sucking each one.

He nibbled on her belly button, the creases on her inner thighs, placing passion marks on the inside of her legs. Mel's body lit up in passion as she squirmed about, her body threatening to have an orgasm simply from his kiss. He was fucking her mind and it was like no other feeling she'd ever experienced.

He continued down the front of her thighs and Mel almost screamed when he kissed her knee caps. She never knew there were so many sensitive places on her body; places that set her on fire.

Connors lifted her foot to the top of his chest, leaned in and placed the head of his jimmy at the opening of her mommy. He eased it inside her, stopping at the rim of his jimmy and just working the tip in and out of her, teasing her. as he wrapped his lips around her pedicured toes. Mel grabbed her hair inside her hands, trying to contain the intensity of the sexual pressure mounting inside her.

"Not yet," he told her as he rolled her over onto her stomach. He again started at the top of her neck, nibbling and biting his way down her back to her ass. He spread her cheeks apart and began sucking the napc of her ass between intense bites to her cheeks. Slowly he moved his way down to the small pink opening. He curled his tongue, forced it inside her ass and Mel dug her nails into the blanket and mat below.

"Oh my god," she moaned, arching her back up off the floor.

Connors pulled her to her knees and buried his face in her ass as he ravished her mommy with his fingers; her ass opening up to receive his tongue. Her river flowed down onto his fingers and Connors wanted to taste it. He turned her back onto her back, grabbed her legs and rolled her up into a ball with her knees planted on the mat beside her ears.

187

With her mommy in the air, wide open and free, he stuck his tongue down inside her, rotating from her mommy to her ass, back and forth. Mel's body began to spasm, experiencing multiple orgasms for the first time in her life. Her legs began to shake violently and her eyes rolled into the back of her head.

She couldn't control what was happening to her body; she screamed out and Connors quickly grabbed his black wife beater from his pile of clothing and placed it in her mouth. As she tried to recover, he slammed down inside her, lifting her pelvis off the mat and fucked her like he had never fucked her before; a perfect mixture of soft to hard, slow to fast, gentle to violent thrusts.

When he felt himself about to nut, Connors pulled Mel up to him and leaned back onto his shins. Mel locked her legs around his waist and gyrated against the pulsating harness of his jimmy. He kissed her and Mel loved the taste and smell of her juices on his lips and face.

"You my bitch right, huh? Tell daddy you his bitch."

"I'm yo' bitch daddy. Oh shit I'm yo' bitch. I'll always be," she said kissing him as he exploded up inside her.

They had a death grip on one another and as they fell down onto the mat, Connors kept Mel wrapped in his arms.

"You trust me don't you?" he asked her, trying to slow his pounding heart.

"Yes."

"Good, I need you to trust me that everything will be alright, can you do that?"

"With my life," she told him.

Connors lay next to her, knowing that he had to figure out how to pull this off, down to every tiny detail as not to get caught. With only one week left on rotation, he also knew he had to move fast but Connors and Mel was about to find out that things don't always go as planned.

The Cincinnati city atmosphere seemed to look so differently to Charlene as she rode along the busy downtown streets on the bus. She hadn't been home in over four years and to see her hometown from the Smokey grey tinted windows was met with many mixed emotions.

The uncertainties of the "free world" was often an uphill battle for many inmates returning home. A hill many were too afraid to climb without the crutches of the world. Without the stability of the structure of confinement, life on the outside sometimes possessed a challenge. It wasn't as hard as it seemed to get used to "3 hot and a cot," no matter how short the stay.

Having a fixed schedule to follow, telling you when you are allowed to do life's simple things such as when to sleep, when to eat, when to work, when you can shower, and even when you can go outside, in some ways becomes as habit forming as when you were a child… it conformed you to a routine. So coming home to open choices could be a very scary thing, especially when one wrong choice could very easily land you back where you don't wanna be.

The unknowns swarmed Charlene's mind… would she be able to find a job, would she be able to handle probation… she'd heard all the horror stories concerning gung ho PO's out to make an example of certain people with certain cases. More so than anything Charlene wondered where she would stay. She had plans to reunite with her family as soon as she was able to leave the halfway house and considering the heart wrenching circumstances she'd endured over her final eighteen months at the hands of Tucker, it made not coming home to the awaiting arms of Marco all the more painful.

All she had known from the moment her and Marco hooked up was him and soon after, the family they had built together. That feeling of security was no longer there and realizing that, Charlene felt so naked now and so alone without the women in prison she had come to rely upon. This journey she would have to walk alone. No Nikki, no Tae, no one could climb this mountain for her. Charlene would have to somehow find the strength in her own hiking boots of faith.

The man she'd loved all those years had made it clear to her that he had moved on and she had to make the decision to do so as well. How, would be a matter of day-by-day will and determination.

As her size 7 Nike hit the grey and white speckled concrete below, Charlene inhaled a deep breath of the Ohio fresh air. It felt so refreshing filling her lungs; not that the camp was all that bad but sometimes even though outdoors, it could threaten to smother you.

She stood there, her cardboard box in her arm looking out across the terminal when she heard the sound of approaching screams in the distance. Charlene allowed the box to fall to the ground as Kayla and Marco Jr., now ten and seven years old, leaped into her arms. Even though she had seen them on visits over the years, somehow watching them come towards her, they seemed to have grown so much and as excited as she tried to be, her heart couldn't help but feel a little sad.

She had missed so much in the time she was away; time that no matter what she Charlene could never got back. Tears began to well up in her eyes once again but these were somewhat tears of joy as she hugged them. She tried her best to put any trace of negative thoughts from her head and just embrace the moment. She could now hold her children free from someone looking over her shoulders. Their touch truly did allot to lift her spirits and as she kissed them repeatedly on their cheeks, she felt that she was ready to face any adversity that came her way, no matter the source… if only for that moment.

Charlene's mother Rosalie walked up to her daughter and threw her arms around her baby girl.

"Welcome home Lena. God has smiled on us today."

"I don't know about all that Ma, it seems that He kinda snickered with a few crooked teeth."

"Just because a smile isn't perfectly straight doesn't make it any less beautiful or enjoyable. You have to get past whatever this fog is surrounding you; every challenge that's about to present itself to you. If not for you then for these two right here. You have way too many things going on right now to trip off any man and anything else that is not of a positive nature. You have a life to rebuild Lena and it starts right here, right now.

You need to remember how many you left behind in that place that don't have this opportunity that God has placed before you."

Charlene looked down to her children and then back to her mother.

"You right Ma, I know I do. So," she inhaled. "I have two hours before I have to check into the halfway house. Can we get a bite to eat?"

As Rosalie drove through the Cincinnati streets, Charlene's mind drifted to Tucker and the impending investigation. She was wondering should she tell her mom about what she went through but decided against it. There was no need to put that weight on her shoulders. The Feds had ensured her that he would be prosecuted to the fullest extent of the law. *Yes*, there a part of her that wished she could've just left the memories of him and the mental torture he'd put her through behind in Kentucky but Charlene knew that had she done that, Tucker wouldn't have stopped.

"What if the next one he tries it with ain't as strong as you are Lena? What if she has no family at all waiting for her out there, no friends to visit or no mail coming in? What if she is already on the edge and she harms herself, maybe even kills herself? We've seen it happen Lena. Do you want that on your conscience? He's a nasty filthy rat Lena, that gave you the perfect poison to kill his ass... now exterminate the bastard Lena!"

Charlene chuckled at the thought of her friend. She always kept Charlene from losing it. She missed her wit and silliness so much already. She always gave Charlene another way of looking at things. Prison wisdom was found in few but proclaimed by many. Her heart ached for Nikki. A crime, although committed, it's debt had been paid three times over when it came to Nikki. Her life had been stripped away and whether she knew or not that it was her husband on the other side of that door when she fired his weapon, in Charlene's eyes, Nikki had long paid her dues to society.

She wanted a life for her friend. One filled with family for the holidays, another chance at love with a good man, a few children... every woman should have the opportunity to feel what she felt the moment her babies leaped into her arms. She felt a tear fall down her face but as she felt her mother touch her knee and heard Kayla's voice in her ear, she snapped back.

"Momma wait until you meet my teacher, she..."

Kayla's fading voice was a much needed jolt to her soul.

I gotta snap outta this, she told herself. Her emotions were all over the place. Somehow she had to find her way.

"Oh before I forget," her mother told her, reaching down in her purse. "This is for you. Marco asked me to bring it to you," she told her, handing her the red envelope.

Charlene looked down at the envelope and took it from her mother's hand. She ripped the top half of the red paper and pulled out a card.

I never meant to hurt you, the card began and that was all it took for her to break.

I know you don't believe me when I say I'm sorry. I never meant for this to happen. Things with her just kinda became a lil normal after a while... and Lena I need something normal in my life with you away. I never wanted to see you go away from me; never wanted the kids to be without you. You've at least gotta know that. Now that you're home I know that finally they can be complete again.

Don't think I have nor will I ever forget the sacrifice you've made for me and our family and even though things aren't how it was planned to be... I'll always love you Lena, nothing or no one can ever change that. Here's a lil somethin' for you and I hope you know that no matter what my situation is, I'm gonna always come runnin' when you call.

One Luv

Marco

Charlene spread the cash in her hands and counted 50 one hundred dollar bills.

"Five grand Ma?"

"He wanted for you to be able to get clothes and anything else you needed. He's been working allot of overtime to save that for you. That's why I've had the kids so much... well, between me and Tiffany."

Charlene wiped her face and looked to her mother.

"It's crazy Ma," Lena chuckled. "You knew huh? You knew he had no plans to be with me and you didn't say a word? How could you look me in the face during all those visits and keep that from me? Knowing my life was gonna fall apart the moment I walked out of there."

"He asked me not to say anything Lena," she said, pulling the car over. "Nobody, especially me wanted to see you deal with this while you were still in there. I wanted you to be able to focus on getting back out here to your babies and for that, I'll never apologize.

Now if Marco had my grandchildren around someone who mistreated them or didn't take care of them then by all means, I would have stepped in and it would've been addressed, you know that. But from what I can see baby she takes really good care of them. Do they seem like they're unhappy? I mean honestly Lena, look at them. Because at the end of the day, is that not what's most important?"

Charlene sighed a deep sigh. Her feelings were so conflicted at that moment. Marco had constantly told her that he was working and Charlene constantly accused him of lying, which probably pushed him closer to Tiffany. When all along, he was working so she could be okay when she came home, regardless of the fact that they wouldn't be together. *How was she supposed to feel?*

"When he kept saying he was workin' I just knew he was lying. I kept giving him all kinds of grief about not coming to visit with the kids. Come to find he was working to stack some cash for me?" she said, holding the envelope up in the air.

When she jerked the envelope a gold key fell down into her lap. Charlene looked down at the small piece of metal glistening in the sunlight. She picked up the key and looked at her mom.

195

"What's this?"

"It's your door key. To a three bedroom townhouse over on Hetz Ave. Lena, it's fully furnished and all your things have been brought over. The phone has been turned on already so that once you're able to go home, the kids will be able to stay the weekends with you," she told Charlene, rubbing her tears from her face.

"Are you kidding Ma? You and dad didn't have to…"

"I didn't. Your dad and I was going to but then we were told not to."

"Marco?" she whispered.

Her mother shook her head. Charlene took a deep breath and gripped her chest. She didn't know how to take all of it in. Marco had made sure that most of her worries were gone. Thanks to him, she had a furnished home with her children, money to start over and all of her most treasured things already awaiting her.

If she wasn't so heartbroken over him leaving her, she would be so excited, yet without him in Charlene's mind, nothing seemed as good.

"We're here in front of your favorite restaurant. Let's just worry about all the woulda, coulda and shoulda's later. Right now, let's take the little time you have and spend it making a memory with your babies."

Charlene looked in the back seat to her two children who were playing with one another and talking back and forth to her. Yes, she would make the best of this hour and a half she had with her babies. She'd worry about everything else later. Really she couldn't wait to talk to Nikki about everything that was going on. Charlene loved her mother with all her heart but she had been with

Charlene's dad for over forty years, so Charlene couldn't imagine that she could understand how she was feeling.

She'd call Nikki as soon as she had gotten settled in the halfway house, she told herself as she exited her mother's Cadillac. She opened the back door as her bundles of joy hopped out and grabbed their mother's hand.

For a moment nothing else mattered as she looked down at her children, one on each side of her, arms swinging with hands locked inside of hers. Tiffany or no Tiffany, she was their mother and yes, Tiffany may have been there for a few of those nights that she couldn't but she was home now and as she down looked at the ringing cell phone her mother was holding out to her, Charlene vowed that she'd be the one from that day on out, that would fill those nights.

"It's for you, it's Marco."

Connors thought long and hard about how to make Mel's abortion happen and it all came down to one simple conclusion, everything had to be as discreet as possible. There was no trusting anyone other than Mel and himself.

One by one, he thought through every detail. He played out every scenario that could arise and he put together a counter active solution. First he found an abortion clinic that was a nonprofit and accepted patients with little or no insurance; one whose privacy policy was its top priority.

He found a *Birthright* clinic on Nicholasville Road in Lexington. Next he addressed the issue that Mel wouldn't have any identification other than the one that listed her prison ID number. So for the day he had made her appointment, Connors has taken his wife's driver's license from her tan Michael Kors purse on the chocolate brown marble kitchen countertop.

Mel and his wife looked nothing alike other than the fact that their skin tone was close in color; this made him a little uneasy so the day before her appointment he went to the local beauty supply and purchased her a wig that looked similar to the short bobbed hairstyle she wore on her license.

He asked Mel her size in clothing and went to the local Citi Trends and bought her an outfit to help her blend in as opposed to wearing the prison bought light grey t-shirt and shorts. Her appointment was set for ten am and Mel needed help to ensure that she could get off the compound undetected and safely. She enlisted the help of Ella to pull it off.

According to the plan, at nine am Ella was to complain of having chest pains and while staff and medics were attending to her. Mel, who would be exercising up and down the hill outside, would then run across the parking lot and hop into an awaiting car that Connors had rented for the occasion.

Mel wouldn't have to be accounted for until four pm standing count so that gave them roughly five and a half hours to get the procedure done. With the plan in place, right on schedule, Ella made her way to the officer's station and began to gasp for breath and clutch her chest, telling the officer she was having difficulty breathing. The tall white female quickly grabbed her radio from her waist and called for help. Office personnel, medical staff and the perimeter guard were to respond. Ella put on a grand show allowing Mel to get to the bottom of the hill unseen by both nosey inmates and the perimeter truck.

She ran across the road, through the empty parking lot of the Recreation center and into the awaiting red Saturn's back driver's side door. Her heart was pounding as she ducked down between the front and back seats. Connors had been at the Rec center for the past hour working out so that if he was seen leaving the premises there was no suspicion.

Mel pulled the door closed and Connors pulled off the parking lot. As they headed up the hill and passed the pavilion, the ambulance for Ella was coming up the main road. He decided to sit at the crossing and allow it to pass by before proceeding to turn onto the road and risk the up high occupants of the emergency vehicle to see down inside his back seat. As he sat at the three-way crossing, the perimeter truck heading over to the men's facility pulled up next to him on the driver's side of his car waiting for the emergency vehicle to pass as well.

When Connors noticed the truck approaching behind him, he whispered for Mel to stay down nice and low.

When the white Ford F-250 stopped beside him, the officer let down his window, leaned over to his passenger side seat and spoke to Connors who shifted in his seat nervously.

"What's going on over there?" Connors asked him, trying to be nonchalant.

Mel was sweating bullets on the back seat floor trying her best to stay down virtually underneath front seats.

"Somebody had a heart attack," the officer responded.

Connors was so nervous but once the perimeter guard bid him farewell, he made a right turn and headed down the main road, through the brick entrance and down Leestown Road.

"That was too close for comfort. Stay down baby until I tell you we clear."

Mel agreed as she slumped down over the middle hump of the back floor. Connors turned on the radio as he headed down the road past the VA Medical Center and crossed the exchange where Leestown turned to W. Main Street.

Mel lay her head on the ledge of the back seat unsure of how she felt. She understood that this had to happen but she had to admit that there was a part of her that wished it didn't. She closed her eyes and felt the road underneath the sedan. It had been almost a year since she'd seen scenery other than that of the camp grounds.

She looked up and out the back window at the sky, her hand rubbing her stomach. Her thoughts drifting to the life she held inside her; the life of a child she shared with the man she loved to death.

As Aaron Hall played over the car speakers, Mel tried her best not to think of the impending procedure she wished with all her heart she didn't have to endure.

"... when you need me, I will be right by your side. When you need me, I will be there. Before you can call me. When you need me, you won't have to worry or cry cause when you need me, I will be there..."

Mel felt her eyes began to water and as if in sync with her emotions, Connors reached to the back seat and began reaching for her hand. Mel locked her fingers inside his and Connors told her that he loved her.

"It's gonna be aight Melody, I promise baby," he said, rubbing his thumb across the back of her hand.

"... I was blessed the day I found you, sometimes I just can't believe that someone like you so beautiful, could stay with someone like me..."

Mel wanted so badly to beg him to turn the car around and not make her go through with it. She squeezed his hand.

"...So whatever made us down in the past, let's put all that behind. Cause what we have right now, is a sacred vow. I'll be with you, I'll be with you oh baby... when u need me..."

Connors pulled up into the apartment complex in the 600 block of West Main Street and pulled around the brick townhomes to the back parking lot next to the blue waste dumpster. He got out of the car and went into the trunk, grabbed the bag of things he bought for her and walked around to the passenger side rear door.

"...you and I, is all that we need. So baby let's not look nowhere else baby for love..."

He opened the car door and handed her the black plastic bag and stood guard outside smoking a cigarette as she changed into the wig and outfit he'd gotten her.

"... I'll be right there for you before you call, I'll be right there for you, I'll hold you all night long. I'll be right there for you, I'll help you ease your pain. I'll be right there for you, I'll be there for you...."

Mel began to sob quietly to herself as she slid her shorts down over her legs.

"... I'll be right there for you to dry your eyes, I'll be right there for you sweet baby don't you cry. I'll be right there for you, I'll love you endlessly. I'll be right there for you, I'll be there for you...."

Once Mel changed, Connors told her to get in the front seat with him. He handed her the small empty purse to complete her ensemble along with his wife's driver's license and as Mel stared down at the pretty face on the license, she found herself beginning to cry again.

Connors returned the gear to *park* and turned to her.

"I'm sorry baby; I know this has to be so hard for you. It's not easy for me either but we've gone too far to turn back now. We're off the grounds now, we're exposed to any and everything that could go wrong now," he told her, pulling her into his arms. "We gotta go finish this, ok? Time is not on our side right now baby, ok?"

Mel reluctantly shook her head in agreement and rode alongside him in silence down Pasadena Blvd., until he brought the car to a stop at the Birthright clinic. When he turned the car off, he looked over to a stoic Mel.

"You ready?"

She looked over to him briefly but she didn't respond. She simply opened the door, stepped out the car, looked around, inhaled a deep breath and closed the door. She looked across the street at the Signature furniture store as she waited for Connors to come around the car. He walked up to her, placed his hands on both sides of her face, leaned in and placed a kiss on her lips.

"You said you trust me right?" he asked her, rubbing her back. Mel shook her head, *yes*.

"Don't stop ok? Take my hand," he told her, extending his hand to her.

Hand in hand across the parking lot, Mel felt saddened by the thought of something so simple as holding hands that under different circumstances would mean the world to her.

He opened the door for her and as soon as she entered the clinic, she had to rush to the bathroom to throw up. The smell of death in the air made her sick. She wanted to leave but as her alias was called to check in, Mel knew that was not an option.

"Karmia Connors?" the receptionist called again, looking around the waiting area.

Connors nudged Mel on the leg.

"You're my wife today remember?"

A nervous Mel went to the receptionist's desk and looked back to Connors as she handed the young, blonde haired woman her fake ID.

"Thank you Mrs. Connors, you can have a seat and we'll call you back shortly," the lady told Mel after taking her signed consent form from her.

As Mel wrote the fictitious name on the paper, she again began to cry.

Mrs. Connors?

The receptionist handed Mel some tissue and patted her hand softly.

"It'll be okay, don't cry. You can have a seat," she told Mel as Connors came up to the desk, took Mel by the hand and led her back to her seat.

He sat next to her, rubbing her hand.

"You must think so low of me right now huh Melody? To go through all this to hold onto my job and family at your expense? If it makes you feel any better, I didn't sleep a wink last night, wondering if I'm doing the right thing, by you and by God."

Mel looked up to him through her reddened eyes.

"The truth is, this is my wife's third pregnancy. We've had two miscarriages and she is so scared that her body will reject this one as well. So she's been extra careful about what she does and doesn't do. Sex has been pretty much non-existent and for good reason. To be honest, it played a major part in why I got involved with you and that wasn't fair to you.

I know now that while I was tryin' so hard not to hurt her with all she's been through I totally disregarded you and all you've been going through. I've placed you in a horrible position and from the bottom of my heart Melody, I'm so sorry. I was being selfish, only thinking of myself. My wants and needs but... but I *need* you to know that when I tell you that I love you, that I've truly, truly grown to love what you are to me, I mean that. If I could go back," he said, squeezing her hand.

The receptionist called out for her and Mel looked back at him once again as she stood to leave.

"Like you said, we've come too far, going back is not an option."

Connors sat back in the chair and hung his head. He regretted the outcome of his infidelity but he also questioned his eagerness to get rid of what may be his only chance at fatherhood with his wife's inability to carry children to term. Yet as he headed outside to smoke, he wondered how the child Mel was carrying could be a gift from God after he had went against his morals and more so, his vows.

He felt genuinely bad for hurting someone who had been hurt enough in life and it didn't matter if she had come on to him or not, he had the option to be the man he vowed to be and walk away. Yet walking away from Mel wasn't easy for him to do because he felt like a different man in her presence and that fact alone also made him begin to question his love for his wife.

It wasn't just the sexual aspect either he had come to realize; it was her wit, her silliness, her knowledge of things that interested him such as politics. He inhaled his cigarette as Mel lay on the table, feet placed in leg irons and tears running down her face. She tucked her arms under the white cotton blanket and looked around the cold subtle room. It looked like a cheap operating room; no warmth, no life inside.

She tried to block out the sounds of all the metal instruments being placed on the table at her feet.

"You seem really upset, are you sure this is what you want to do?" the female nurse asked her.

Mel looked off to the wall and mumbled.

"I have to save my husband's wife."

She closed her eyes as she felt the needle sting of the local anesthetic being injected into her cervical walls. She closed her eyes and tried to take her mind to another place; a place where things didn't hurt so much all the time. She drifted off and when she felt the soft hand touch her arm to wake her, it was over. The child that bound them together was no more.

When Connors entered the room to assist her to the car, Mel didn't know exactly how to feel. She knew she wasn't angry at him for having to protect home, she was just hurt that things couldn't be the way she wished they could be. Once again, it confirmed Ella's words to her... it was reality and no matter how much she wished she could change it, she couldn't. Once they arrived at the camp, she would have to go to her room and deal with the changes alone; he on the other hand was going home to the woman who was allowed to share in the joy of having a child with him.

The walk up the hill was a little hard for Mel as the anesthetic began to wear off. Before he let her out of the car Connors had told her again that he was sorry and that he loved her. He also told her that he'd bring her some stronger pain pills that night when he arrived on duty.

"Just rest aight," he told her as she returned all the things he'd brought her to the bag and put in the back seat. "If you need somethin', let someone else get it for you, ok?"

Mel struggled up the concrete hill as Connors stayed behind to make sure the coast was clear before he left. When she finally made it to the building, Mel stopped by Ella's room to let her know she was back safely only to find that Ella had actually been taken to the hospital with actual chest pains.

In the process of Mel's plan, Ella was so worried about Mel that she had a panic attack, which for a seventy two year old woman could be just as deadly.

Mel worked her way to her room and over to her bunk. Slowly and gingerly she climbed up the ladder and lay down staring out the window, worrying about Ella and thinking about Connors and his words to her earlier.

She also had regrets but there was nothing that could've went differently. She loved him and had never set out to complicate his life in any way. She just wanted a piece of him and now she was forced to accept that that was exactly all she could ever have... a piece.

Mel looked over to her locker at the Bible Ella had given her. As she tried to climb down and retrieve it, she felt a sharp penetrating pain in her abdomen. Mel tried to breathe through it as she made it to the locker, grabbed the book from the locker top and headed back towards her bunk.

As she neared her bed she clutched the book against her stomach as another violent pain shot down her body.

Mel crumbled onto her Bunkie's bed almost in tears. Something was wrong... very wrong.

Charlene walked into the Landcaster Community Transition Center. Her mother had packed her a few bags so she mostly had everything she needed. Once she was assigned a room she dropped her things on the twin sized bed and went out into the hallway to use the phone. It was close to ten pm count so Charlene felt it was best that she wait until after count.

In the meantime, she unpacked her things and when she came across the card Marco gave her, she read it over and over again. She looked off to the wall and thought back to the conversation they had over the phone as she walked inside the restaurant with their children .

"I wanted to make sure you were good. I know I can't take away all yo' stress but I didn't like the way our last conversation ended. I know this ain't easy for you to deal with, with everything else you got on yo' plate but Lena I'm gone always make sure you good, at least to the best of my ability."

"Thank you," Charlene told him softly, her breath seemingly trapped in her chest. "I know that put allot on you doing that for me but thank you for caring enough to have me somewhere to stay."

"I fully intend for the kids to come live with you as soon as you able and I know you gotta get a job to get that crackin' so… well," he paused, knowing Charlene may not take the next part all too well. "Well Tiff's cousin has her own home health care company and you can start work anytime you ready, so you can get up outta there."

Tiff's cousin?

Charlene looked down to the phone, over to her mom who was avoiding looking back at her, then back down to the phone. She knew that Marco and her mom had discussed her coming home in every detail.

"I want you to fly free Lena, away from the restrictions and be able to move how you want. I know you, so I know the look on your face right now but just think of it as a steppin' stone and make it work for you. You don't gotta respond right now, just think about it aight? I love you Lena."

He hung up.

Charlene finished unpacking and cleaning up her space. She looked to her watch and finally it was time to call the one person she knew would keep it 100 with her and give her the jolt she needed to get herself on track.

"I miss you so already boo, o-m-g I know you got so much to tell me and girllll... have I got juice for you! I'll go first in case I gotta hang up quick. So we at mail call, me and Tae, we chillin' against the wall, when about seventeen Feds come up in this muthafucka, guns drawn talkin' bout everybody stand up against the wall.

We like what the fuck? Then they slam Tucker's bitch ass against the wall, cuff him and read him the script. Girrrllll, I think he pissed himself," she laughed.

Charlene smiled to herself knowing that Tucker would finally feel what it was like to have his freedom stripped away and have to deal with assholes like himself.

"Oh my God bitch you coulda bought him for a dolla."

"Damn what I wouldn't give to have been there to see that shit!"

"Yes, they told him he was charged with rape! Everybody lookin' around like, who he rape? I'm so glad you up out this muthafucka. So now tell me, what happened when you saw your boo when you stepped off that bus?

Charlene leaned back against the wall and filled Nikki in on all the day's events; from Tiffany to the kids, to the money, to her door key.

"You shittin' me right? No he didn't wait till you was thirty-six seconds from freedom to let you know he feelin' some type of way. Girl men are a hot damn mess but on the other side of that Lena, you gotta admit he still held you down. I know you don't wanna hear that shit but it's real talk.

The average niggah that didn't give a fuck woulda just left you out there. He worked double time to make sure you was good. Despite his fuck up. He still in love with you, he just got caught up in a situation he can't just walk away from cause you touched down.

He don't know what's up with you yet boo. He know the Lena you once were but it's been a minute and he basically gotta get to know you all over again. You gotta respect that. He don't know what you on yet. Are you gone get out there and clown, fuck up yo' probation, come back to this hell hole or are you gonna handle yo' business?

He don't know the answers to that, so it's gone take some time Boo but please believe that apartment wasn't rented just for you and the kids. He planned for a future with you. He just wanna make sure you're the same Lena that left him; mark my words Boo. And as far as the job, bitch to get outta there I'd be a yes ma'am, how you like yo' pussy washed askin' bitch!"

They burst out laughing. Charlene knew Nikki would put things in perspective as always. She had the wisdom of an old soul and the feistiness of a young soldier. She understood love and life in a way that made you want to believe in what she said.

"I'm not saying sit around and wait on his ass either. He let you know he love you and he got yo' back, true... but I ain't gone never tell you to sit around and twiddle yo' thumbs while he decides to play house. You move on with yo' life as well. If it's meant to be Lena, it'll be... until then, bitch you got the whole world at yo' feet; go out there and enjoy it, you hear me?"

"I hear you... and you right. I mean my babies was so happy to see me and all they talked about was me meeting teachers and coming to cheer practice. I can't wait to do all those things plus the simple things like comb my baby's hair, ya know?"

"No but I can imagine. Now I gotta go, it's smoke time. I'll turn the phone back on after I come back inside. Call me later if you need me. You know you my bitch right?"

"Right and left," Charlene responded, blowing a kiss though the receiver.

"Don't disappear Lena... ok?"

"Never... I love you Nikki."

"Love you too Lena... now go be great."

Charlene went to her room, sat back on her bed and thought about the job offer Marco had extended to her.

Use it for what it's worth.

The next day, Charlene met with her counselor and explained to her that she had a job lined up that she could begin any day, a home waiting for her and basically all her ducks in a row.

211

"Sounds like somebody has an awesome support system. Consider yourself very lucky. From my many years of experience, I learned that most women become repeat offenders very quickly without one. So it doesn't matter what hoops you gotta jump through, what role you gotta play to hold onto it, that's what you have to do until you can do it on your own, am I clear?"

Charlene shook her head in agreement. Personal hang-ups and feelings would have to go on the back burner for the time being and she would have to grin and bear whatever came her way in order to stay out on the streets.

One thing she knew for sure was that she couldn't allow anything to take away the look on her children's faces as she sat across form them at the restaurant table the day before; looks of pride, admiration and love.

So with that attitude, Charlene over the next thirty days, began working at the home health agency, began taking weekend passes to her apartment which allowed her to spend time with the children, family and even Marco stopping by from time to time.

He'd purchased her a 2010 Ford Focus to get back and forth to work in and to be able to pick up the kids on weekends to give her mother a break. She was also able to attend a lot of the children's functions and it was at one of these events that Charlene finally came face-to-face with Tiffany, Marco's live in girlfriend.

Charlene had often wondered how she'd react when she finally laid eyes on her. Would she be angry? Bitter? She simply didn't know. Marco had for the most part kept her out-of-sight from Charlene, whether dropping the kids off or at functions.

This was the woman who had literally taken her place in the family she had dedicated her life to building. Yet surprisingly, face-to-face, Charlene showed poise and tact. She complimented her on the job she'd done with the children.

"I know it's not easy to step in and help raise someone else's children. For a minute I was bothered by that but then I had to remember what mattered the most and for me, that was the fact that they were safe and well cared for. For that, I truly thank you from the bottom of my heart."

Charlene then walked away, head held high, hand in hand with her children and smiling to herself. Now everyone knew... momma was home.

Within the following sixty days, Charlene was discharged from the halfway house, living fulltime in her apartment, working a new full time job as a secretary her dad had gotten for her at PNC Bank and attending classes part time at nearby Kaplan University, studying Business Management.

With everything seeming to fall into place in her life, nothing was bigger than the weekend her children finally arrived to live with her permanently. As the U-haul backed up to the apartment complex, Charlene's heart began to flutter. This was the moment she had been waiting for. She flung the apartment door open, ran down the black railed stairs, down to the black top concrete of the parking lot. Marco jumped out the driver's side and his younger brother Sam hopped out the passenger side.

Sam walked back to Charlene and swooped her up in his arms.

"So good to see you sis, welcome home."

Marco smiled at the two of them holding one another, locking eyes with Lena for what felt like an eternity to her. She loved him something awful but she had also gone on a few dates; aiming to get on with her life. She had made it clear to herself that if in fact he was gone, she was ready and able to move forward on her own... or so she thought.

Playful giggles, lingering smiles, flirtatious comments, casual bumps into one another and re-visiting countless memories in conversation filled the day and by the time Marco and Sam left to return the truck, Charlene knew getting over him... truly building a life without him would not be easy.

As she unpacked the boxes in the kid's room, Charlene began to feel a little emotional as she pulled out one of Marco's Lebron James' jersey from the box.

Must've packed it by mistake, she told herself, bringing the jersey up to her nose.

She could smell his body scent throughout the white shiny material and inhaling it caused a surge of electricity to shoot down between her legs. Charlene removed the white wife beater she had on along with the black lace boy shorts and slipped on Marco's jersey. She stood in the mirror and ran her hands across her body. It wasn't the touch she longed for but the overpowering smell was driving her crazy.

She grabbed her cell phone from the dresser, put on some lip gloss, straightened her hair and stood in front of the full length mirror to snap a photo. She sent one to Nikki, one to Tae and the other to Marco.

You accidently pk'd this with MJ's things.

She laid the phone down and lay back on the bed. She'd been home more than two months but still hadn't felt the pleasure of a man so she did what she learned to master while locked down... pleasure herself.

With one hand spreading her lips apart, she wet the tip of her index finger with her tongue and gently massaged her clit as she inhaled Marco's scent and fucked him timelessly in her mind. As she released her orgasmic want for him, her phone began to sing.

214

Bitch you wearing that jersey. I was abt 2 txt u 2. I got the money u sent 2day. U so fuckin' tru to me and I Luv you!! I sent u pics & a letter 2day, the contents will blow ur mind, swear! XOXOX

Tae's popped through with a different tone.

Fuck dat jersey and dat front view, Send dat ass from da bk & raise dat front view abt 12ins...lol. Miss u Boo! Luv u tru!

Charlene laughed. Those two were the best thing she took away from the entire prison experience. She sat the phone down as another message popped up. It was from Marco.

Not an accident... if u keep diggin' u'll c why.

Charlene looking puzzled at the text, sat the phone back onto the dresser and walked back over to the brown cardboard box on Kayla's bed and began searching deeper through the articles of clothing only to find several of Marco's things.

You Got Mail... her phone sung again.

The more I see u... the more I realize I love u, I need u and I can't be w/o u... I've missed u so fuckin' much Lena and...

Marco quietly slid his key in the front door, crept inside and gently closed it behind himself.

Charlene felt her eyes well up with tears. *Could it really be? What was he trying to tell her? Was he really planning to leave Tiffany in the future?*

No, not the future... in his mind he'd been gone the moment he laid eyes on Lena at the school. The confidence she displayed commanded his attention; it let him know that she was the lady of their family and she home to reclaim her thrown. He saw the Lena

215

he once fell in love with, come home and grind, the same way she used to; to make sure that her family was good. He wanted her back and as he looked down at the text coming back through, he knew he'd do whatever it took to make that happen.

And what?

"And I wanna come home," he told her, resting in the doorway of Lil' Marco room, looking at her, standing in the middle of the room wearing his jersey.

He walked over to Charlene, took the phone from her, snatched her into his arms and kissed her with a passion neither had ever felt come from one another before. He grabbed the clip from her hair, releasing it and gripped it inside his fist as Charlene dug her nails into his back.

He picked up from the floor, her legs wrapping around his waist and sat her down on the tan colored oak dresser. Charlene began to unbuckle his black leather Michael Kor belt and then his black Levi jeans. Marco pulled back from her.

"I'm sorry Lena... I never... I never meant...," he said, a tear falling from his eye onto her thigh.

Charlene's heart broke to see him hurting. She wiped his eyes and told him she forgiven him.

"We went through all this for a reason. Maybe to get us away from that lifestyle so we could understand the importance of being around for our kids. Not taking anything for granted, including each other. I love you baby, I always have and no matter what I'll never stop."

Marco swallowed her up in his kiss, lavishing her with his love for her. His phone began to vibrate. He looked down at the scene to find Tiffany calling. Charlene wiped the corners of his mouth and asked him if he needed to take that or to leave.

"Not at all, she just came home to find the key on the counter with a note explaining why it's there and an empty closest in the bedroom where my clothes used to be."

He kissed her on her lips and nodded towards the excess boxes around them.

"I'm never going anywhere again. We in this for life, feel me?" he said reaching in his back pocket and pulling out the small black velvet box.

Charlene's eyes brightened and began to water as he opened it, revealing a beautiful platinum engagement ring.

"I've hurt you and so I understand if you don't want to answer this right now. But I wasn't sure who the Lena was that was coming back after being away. I saw a side of you that I guess the environment in there brought out of you and so I wasn't sure how it would be, how you would be but when I saw you.... When I saw you at Kayla's award ceremony I saw you. I saw my Lena and knew I wanted her back in my life... forever. You can take some time and think about it but I would love it if..."

"I don't need to think... yes... the answer is, has and will always be yes!"

The love they made that evening wasn't make up sex or desperation sex... it was the cementing of a bond that had stood one of the most difficult tests of time and as she lay in his arms, Charlene realized that had she not responded to the situation the way she had and accepted her responsibility for her part in the situation, she wouldn't be laying next to her future husband.

Her life had come full circle and she owed to one person. As she took a picture of her 3 Karat diamond ring on her finger and hit send, she included one simple sentence… *you were right*!

She smiled as Nikki responded.

He ain't want that pussy out there runnin rampant…lhh! U go bitch!!! I'm so happy 4 u and I love u, I love u, I love u!!

Charlene tossed the phone to the side and lay her head back on Marco's chest, snuggling under the blanket Nikki gave her with the man she thought she'd never have again… home.

Kelly showered and dressed in one of Tae's t-shirts before bouncing down on the grey, black and white striped couch and propped her feet underneath her. She had worked nearly twelve hours that day covering someone's shift at the clinic. The best part of her day was cuddling up on the couch, under her favorite bright orange, pink and white blanket Tae had someone make for her at the camp and await Tae's daily after count phone call.

As she waited by the phone, she shifted through the pile of mail she picked up from the doorway when she arrived home. When she came upon the light purple envelope addressed to her from the Leestown Road address. Her eyes widened as she kissed the front of the envelope. She always loved receiving letters from Tae; sure phone calls were nice but they were short and Tae often couldn't say what she wanted to say since the calls were recorded and the phones were stationed less than a foot from the next. Inside her letters, she always took the time to express her feelings in greater detail.

Songs for her to listen too which Tae told her described her love for her; sexual scenarios that Tae told her they were going to experience when she came home, which thankfully wasn't that far ahead.

Kelly ripped open the envelope, took a sip of her Manischewitz red wine and unfolded the folded yellow papers. Instantly she knew something was wrong, as she noticed the handwriting on the paper wasn't Tae's. She became nervous praying that someone wasn't writing to inform her that Tae had gotten into some kind of trouble and had been locked down. The author of this letter however had written for a very different reason, to inform Kelly of something else.

Kelly

You don't know me but as you can see I definitely know you. For the past sixteen months or so, we have been sharing the love of the same woman... Taedra.

From the moment we left the transfer facility in Oklahoma, we have been inseparable. From a shower together our first night at the camp to the night she lay with me against her chest, her stroking my face with her finger (I know, her signature move right?) and telling me how much she loved me. The countless nights she made love to me, kissing me from head to toe and using the handmade strap on to further my pleasure. I always thought it was so wonderful how she always went out of her way to satisfy me, don't you agree?

She told me she was your first, mine too. Didn't you find that she was just the perfect one to initiate you into her life of intense sexual pleasure? Her soft lips, the way she likes to pull your clit between her teeth and tickle it with the tip of her tongue, the way she spreads your ass cheeks and nestle her clit up against the crease and ride you... oh no, I forgot, you haven't experienced that one yet. I taught her that but no worries; she LOVES it so I'm sure she will try it on you.

She has meant so much to me and her promises of us being together once she gets home has meant even more. I enclosed some photos for you.

Kelly quickly flicked through the papers until she began to see papers with tons of pictures copied on them; pictures of Tae and a very pretty young woman Kelly could only assume was the author of the horror story she was reading. Page after page, she saw Tae and the unknown women in poses that suggested they knew one another as more than friends. One stood out however; a photo of Tae sitting on a blanket in the grass behind the woman who was lying on her side and her ass right at Tae's waist.

220

Kelly pulled the paper closer and through the falling tears she noticed two things. Tae's necklace and cross draped around the woman's next and the young woman's pussy print which had Tae's finger tips protruding from it. Kelly couldn't believe what she was seeing, especially the cross that she'd returned to Tae through a visit around another woman's neck. She picked back up the letter from the couch.

This letter was not meant to hurt you but to simply inform you that just like the half moon shaped birthmark on the inside of her upper thigh, you know the one, planted perfectly between her pussy lip and the crease of her thigh, I ain't going nowhere sweetie! Looking forward to us ALL sharing one hell of a time some day!

Signed, your future Wife-In-Law

Kelly became sick, her stomach quivering like she had to throw up. She jumped from the couch and ran into the bathroom, feeling her eyes sockets were about to burst as the wine and food she'd eaten, made its way from her guts to the toilet below. Uncontrollably she hurled until she felt her insides tie in knots.

She sat down on the floor, wiping the puke remnants from her mouth with her hand. She began to sob as she thought of how Tae had promised her from day one, she would never hurt her. Why would she do this to me, Kelly asked herself, knowing she had been nothing but faithful to Tae since the day she'd met her; her mother practically disowning her for her choice to be with her. Kelly was devastated

She pulled herself up off the floor as her cell phone began to ring. She staggered to the living room and pushed the letter out the way. It was Tae calling. A million questions began to run through her mind. *Do I answer? What do I say? Do I let her know that I know?*

As livid as she was, Kelly picked up the phone and pressed the answer key.

"Hey Bae," she said, trying to sound as normal as she could.

Tae however wasn't fooled. She could tell something was off.

"What's wrong Bae, you aight?"

"I'm, fine," she lied. "Why do you ask?"

"Come on Bae, who knows you better than me? I know when somethin's different in the sound of yo' voice. You getting sick?"

Kelly looked down at the floor to the various pieces of paper scattered about. She fought to stay composed. *I'm sick alright*, she told herself.

"Yeah, never could fool you huh bae? I must've ate something at work that's not agreeing with me. Got me a lil' queasy," she lied. She didn't want to give Tae a heads up on what she'd just found out.

"Thought so; you know I know that body inside and out. Well I won't hold you too long cause I want you to get some rest," Tae told her, looking to Nikki who was standing outside the phone room waiting for her.

While Kelly was still the love of her life, Tae had to admit that Nikki was coming in at a close second. She respected Tae's feelings for Kelly and that was one of the main reasons she had fallen so hard for Nikki... grown woman shit.

"Yeah, I think I'll just go ahead and lie down, see if I feel better in the morning," Kelly said, holding her hand over her mouth, muffling the sound of her cries.

Tae had never ushered her off the phone before, sick or not, she'd want to talk until the operator said it was time to hang up. She was spoiled that way. Looking at the pieces of paper again, Kelly had to wonder if she woman in the pictures was the reason Tae hurried to hang up.

"Aight bae, you do that. Just rest and get better. I'll check on you tomorrow, love you."

Her words seemed to pour salt in an open wound. *Love me, no you couldn't!*

Kelly got off the phone feeling like her world was crumbling around her. Slowly her hurt turned to anger thinking of how she had waited, stay loyal, made the five hour drive to visit every other weekend, worked overtime shifts to make sure she had money on her books and here of late, risked her own freedom to drop off packages for her at the bottom of the hill when she came to visit.

Kelly was livid as she lay across the bed, crying and staring at the pictures of Tae and the woman she'd betray her with. She felt like such a fool; stupid for ever falling for her and sorry that she had hurt her mother in the process for someone who had just shown her that she never deserved her.

Her next scheduled visit was two days away but Kelly decided to call off work, get up and head out at 3 am to make the drive and arrive bright and early at 8am when visitation began. Tae was in total shock when they sent up to the room for her and informed her she had a visit. She was lying in the bed with Nikki when the knock came at her door.

As Tae showered she thought back over the few months. Her and Nikki had become extremely close and even Bright Eyes had picked up a new fling here and there. Tae was actually happy she'd found a few to occupy her time but every now and then, she'd still find a note from Bright Eyes under her pillow.

As she lathered her body, she reminisced back to the previous night when Bright Eyes had come to her room to say goodbye; she was leaving the following morning. She had come right after 4am count when she knew everyone would be sleeping. She tip-toed by Nikki's room and into Tae's. Meko had her back turned to the doorway so after she entered, she softly closed the door behind her and placed her robe over the window.

Bright Eyes gently climbed up onto the crème colored ladder at the bottom of Tae's bed to her bunk. She removed the white robe she was wearing and began to crawl up between Tae's legs. She began to place a series of soft kisses on Tae's lips and neck. She sent her tongue out to trace the outer rim of Tae's lips as a foggy Tae began to move about underneath the covers.

Her lips responded, her hand began to awake and Tae began to moan at the warm feel of the naked creature lying on top of her. It was dark inside the room but as soon as Tae raised her hand to run her fingers through the silhouette's hair, she knew instantly it wasn't Nikki who towered above her. Tae gripped Bright Eyes by the arms with a death grip.

"What the fuck you think you doin'?"

Bright Eyes pried Tae's right hand from her arm and placed it on her breast.

"I leave in three hours... I ain't never asked you for shit have I? Other than yo' love and since you took that from me, don't take this moment from me too," she said, sliding Tae's other hand down between her legs.

Tae felt the heat and wetness of Bright Eye's want for her illuminating from her mommy. She tried to pull her hand away but Bright Eyes began to glide back and forth against it and Tae could do nothing but shake her head.

224

"I can't do this, stop."

"You can baby," she responded, gliding Tae's fingers underneath her, up inside her mommy. "Nobody's up, everybody sleep. It's just us. You were my first, you broke this pussy in and I want you to be my last. I want to remember the feeling you give me for the rest of my life.... fuck me... fuck me Tae... gimme that good shit... I need it."

Bright Eyes played to Tae's ego and within minutes they were engaged in hot and heated sex, raw and uncut. Tae figured what was one more night before she never had to see or hear from Bright Eyes again? And when the act was done, Bright Eyes simply looked at Tae and said, "I fuckin' love you. Don't come down to see me leave. I want to remember you just like this."

She kissed Tae with a hunger she'd never given before; then grabbed her robe, climbed down her bunk, wrapped her robe around her and walked out the room. Their act of passionate betrayal was mentioned by neither and Bright Eyes walked away knowing that Tae's world was about to come crumbling down soon thanks to the letter she'd dropped in the mailbox three nights prior to her departure.

Got broke off and broke you! Not bad for an immature bitch huh Boo? She chuckled to herself. You have no idea what's about to hit you! Wish like hell I could be here to see the fireworks coming your way Boo.

Tae continued to think of their last hurrah as she dressed. Bright Eyes had undoubtedly brought her some good memories in the months they were together. No one had she'd been with before possessed Bright Eyes' zest for being freaky... no one and those memories she would keep forever.

Kelly sat down at the small square visiting room table twirling the platinum promise Tae had given her around her ring finger. She looked around at all the love ones awaiting their visits. For the first time Kelly looked at the atmosphere differently. She looked at the children playing in the playroom and thought of how much she had been willing to give up to be with Tae. She wondered how many boyfriends or husbands were there under the same false pretenses she'd been all those prior months, thinking that their incarcerated loved ones were being faithful.

The rage inside her began rising but as she saw a surprised Tae come walking into the visiting room smiling ear-to-ear, Kelly put on the best fake smile she could muster up. As she stood up, she straightened the lilac colored t-shirt she was wearing and fixed her Rock Revival Capri diamond studded jeans. She ran her fingers through her hair and opened her arms to receive the hug Tae gave her.

"Damn beautiful," Tae said, looking Kelly up and down. "It's so good to see you baby. I'm glad you feeling better but why you ain't tell me you was coming up here last night?"

"Oh because then, I wouldn't get to see the look you have on your face right now. Tell me Taedra, what exactly is on the other side of that look? Like, what's really behind it? Are you truly happy to see me or a maybe a little unnerved that this visit pulled you away from your little whore upstairs?"

Tae almost choked, trying to swallow the water she'd drank from the bottle Kelly had placed on the table for her before their visit. Kelly always stopped at the vending machine and got Tae's favorites each visit, a Honey Bun, Vienna hot corn chips and a bottled water. Tae returned the top to the bottle and set it back on the table. Her eyes were wide and she was speechless. She didn't know quite how to respond since she didn't know exactly what Kelly knew or was pretending to know. She tried to calm herself.

It could be a test, she told herself. *So let me not put my foot in my damn mouth.*

She calmly asked Kelly what exactly she had meant by the question.

"What you mean what's behind it? How could you even ask me somethin' like that? Bae stop it, what is this that all about? You know you my one and only. Why would you come at me like that? You know me..."

"Save the bullshit Taedra!" she said, her voice beginning to raise in volume. "You think you so fuckin' smooth huh?," she said chuckling to herself and shaking her head.

"I just simply can't fuckin' believe you! All this time you been playin' games with me, when I'm the real bitch that been by yo' side and you fuck me over for some lil' stupid ass hoe up in here? I coulda been off somewhere livin' my fuckin' life! All the shit I took to fuck with you Taedra?"

Tae tried to grab Kelly's hands but she snatched away, continuing to let the words rip from her mouth as visitors and inmates alike looked on in amusement.

"Bae please, keep yo' voice down and calm down. Let me talk to you. Sit down... lets..."

"Fuck sitting down and fuck talking! You had ample opportunity to tell me what the hell you'd been up to all this time but you ain't opened yo' mouth to say shit... so you can keep that shit to yo 'self now! Who the fuck do you think you are, playin' with my life like that?"

The guard came over and warned Kelly that if she didn't sit down and lower her voice she would have to leave. Kelly looked to the small female black woman, across the table at Tae and back to the guard.

"No need, I'm done," she said huffing and puffing, staring Tae in the eyes. "For good."

She reached in her back pocket and grabbed the yellow pieces of paper and pictures. She threw them onto the table before heading towards the door. Tae attempted to go after her but the guard told her she had to sit down. She pleaded with the small female officer to allow her to go after her and talk to her but the guard told her no.

"One more thing," Kelly said, stopping at the door and turning around.

She removed the promise ring from her finger and launched it at Tae's head causing her to duck to keep from getting hit.

"Now the lil' young bitch can rock it along with yo' chain on the next picture!"

Kelly turned and walked out the door as Tae sat in the chair, restrained by the guard, calling after her. She picked up the scraps of paper from the table and the officer told her that her visit was over. Tae would have to wait until she found someone to come down and strip her before she could release her. Tae looked around embarrassingly at everybody both looking at and whispering about her. She knew that this incident would be the talk of the compound as soon as visitation was over. She sat back in the chair took the time she had to read the contents of the letter and felt the tears began to well up in her eyes. Line by line, she read how Bright Eye's had single handed, destroyed her life and future with Kelly.

The letter, the morning before... she had planned it all... and well. Tae felt her heart rip from her chest and there was nothing she could do about it. She knew that there was no way Kelly would come back to her. All she'd ever asked from Tae was her loyalty, the same loyalty she asked of Kelly. She had held up her end of the bargain and as Ms. Crumple came down to strip her out; she had already gotten word as to why Tae's visit had ended so abruptly.

She waved Tae over and the guard took the letter from Tae's hand.

"You know you can't take this with you."

As Tae entered the changing room followed Ms. Crumple, she wiped the tears from her face. Ms Crumple stood in front of her, arms folded and shook her head.

"Don't stand there now with those crocodile tears in yo' eyes. I warned you about this very thing but no, *you do this* right?" she chuckled. "Well now, as you standin' here ballin' like a baby, I ask you, was that bite of the forbidden apple..... was it worth it?"

All Tae could do was drop her head, the tears falling from her eyes. She had lost everything... at least everything that mattered on the outside. And all she could do was shake her head, *no*.

Mel gripped the blanket beneath her in excruciating pain. She didn't know what to do as the small frequently falling beads of sweat poured down her forehead.

The pain she was experiencing was like none she'd ever felt before and she bit down onto the pillow trying not to scream. Her Bunkie came in for standing count and when she noticed Mel hunched over on her bed, she rushed over to her side and asked if she was okay.

Mel couldn't answer, the intensity of the pain overtaking her breath. Her Bunkie noticed small trickles of blood running from the inside of Mel's legs down onto her bed. She'd seen a bad case or two of menstrual cramps but never to this extreme; so she knew this was something else, something very different.

Mel couldn't hold the agony inside any longer and she began to scream out so loud that everyone on the second floor heard her. One by one, they came rushing down the hallway to her room to see what was going on as the blood volume coming from between her legs began to increase.

"Help me somebody, pleaseeeeee…. please help me," she said, grabbing the blanket and pleading at the top of her lungs.

One of the inmates ran down to the officer's station as her roommate sat on the bed beside her, brushing her hair back from her sweaty brow and trying to soothe her as best she could.

The blood from between her legs was pooling at the center of Chell's bed and Chell asked Mel what happened.

"Can you tell me what's wrong Melody? Did someone hurt you? Try and tell what happened?"

No, Mel couldn't do that; no matter how much pain she was experiencing, sharing her secret with anyone was not an option in her mind, not even if it ended up costing her her life.

Mel's blood pressure slowly began to drop and she began to fade in and out of consciousness as the medical staff rushed into the room to attend to her. They moved Chell and the rest of the onlookers from the area. Once the nurse practitioner saw the bloody scene before her, she screamed for the officer to get an ambulance quick.

They started an IV on Mel to get fluids into her body and placed an oxygen mask over her face to help her breathe. There wasn't much they could do besides monitor her vitals until the Paramedics arrived.

Ms. Harlett began asking Chell if she knew what could possibly be wrong with Mel.

"I don't know, she was like that when I got here to the room."

Ms Harlett pulled Chell away from the crowd and began to press her for more information, knowing that the women on the compound, especially those that bunked together shared everything together... especially secrets.

"If you know something, now is the time to speak. Whatever it is that is going on with Inmate Simpson, it is very serious and if you know what it is, you need to tell us so we can help her," Ms. Harlett said, looking at Chell over the rim of her navy blue wire framed glasses.

Ms. Harlett was stern but also fair to the women at the camp. With strong Gospel roots, she encouraged the women to do positive productive things both while they were there and upon completion of their sentence.

She had a no nonsense tolerance for breaking the rules however and as she stood there in front of Chell demanding answers, she knew Chell knew or had a good idea what was going on with Mel, who was now being loaded onto a stretcher semi-conscious.

Chell honestly had no clue though. Mel made sure of that. She kept her business to herself and Chell may have had suspicions like everyone else but she couldn't say with certainty what was happening with her roommate.

"I really don't know Ms. Harlett."

As Mel was being rolled off the elevator on her way out the front door of the camp, they passed Ella who had just returned to the camp from the hospital, sitting in a wheelchair waiting by the officer's station door to check in.

When she saw her prison daughter being rushed out to the awaiting ambulance that had just returned her to the camp, Ella began to holler.

"Wait, wait what's wrong? Where you taking her? What's the matter with her? What's the matter with my baby?"

The officer told Ella she had to calm down before she landed back beside Mel in the ambulance again.

"She started screaming for help in a lot of pain and she's bleeding down there between her legs, a lot. Right now she's in and out of consciousness and she's lost a pretty good amount of blood."

Ella began to sob as the officer checked her back into the camp. She began to call to God for Mel's healing. She was the only one who knew what it could be causing Mel's condition but like Mel, she'd never tell a soul. She refused to jeopardize Mel in any way. Connors she didn't care about but Mel she loved dearly.

All the things that could've went wrong started swirling around in Ella's mind and she tried her best to remain calm. The officer assured her that as soon as she heard any news concerning Mel that she would come and inform her immediately. Ella asked the officer to hand her the Bible from her locker.

Ella opened it to Psalms 23 and began to intercede for the young woman she had come to love just as her own.

"Lord you are her shepherd, her light and salvation. You make her to lie down in green pastures. You restore her soul, yea tho she walks right now through the valley of the shadow of death, we will fear no evil for tho art with us..."

Ella asked God to spare Mel's life, knowing that she had gone through so much and that He had a plan and purpose for her life.

"You've always looked past our faults and saw our needs. I'm askin' you to touch her right now Lord and heal her just as you healed the woman with the issue of blood..."

Mel rode in the ambulance trying to stay awake, so afraid of what was happening to her. She could hear the EMT's asking her to say her name but Mel couldn't bring her mouth to move. The lights from the vehicle's ceiling was flashing in her face with fading views of the EMT and one of the officers from the male facility who was required to ride along to maintain custody of her.

Fading thoughts of Connors flashed through her mind before she lost consciousness altogether. She wanted him near her, to hear him say that everything would be okay just as he had so many times before but as her eyes closed and her breath faded from her chest, the life was seeping from her body and Mel had more pressing things to worry about... survival.

"She coded on the way on but we got her back," the slim white EMT told the awaiting doctor at the University of Kentucky's Good Samaritan Hospital ER entrance.

Mel looked at the ceiling's bright lights, They reminded her of passing through a tunnel. She prayed for a light at the end of the tunnel as they rushed her down the cold corridor and into a trauma room.

They removed the portable oxygen mask from her face and replaced it with a ventilator to breathe for her. Mel saw the already faint images fade altogether. She was given a general anesthesia through her IV that rendered her unconscious allowing them to stabilize her and exam her further.

Clearly from the amount of blood Mel had lost the attending physician thought that he may be dealing with a case of extreme PID (Pelvic Inflammatory Disease) or a fibroid that had caused her to have some severe abdominal bleeding.

It wasn't until he called for an emergency ultrasound that he saw the cause of Mel's illness. On the 11x17 screen, he could see the source of the excessive bleeding; hemorrhaging scar tissue from a recent surgical procedure that had left apart of Mel's womb with the inability of her blood to coagulate.

Mel walking up the hill after she returned from the clinic increased the blood flow to the injured area and the hemorrhaging took over from there.

Their first order of business was to stop the bleeding so Mel was given Antifirinolytic to aide in the clotting of her blood along with a blood transfusion. She was taken to surgery to repair the injured tissue and three hours later, Mel awakened to three Federal agents at her bedside, asking questions concerning a documented aborted pregnancy.

Mel looked around the room at all the machines, the IV's in each of her arms, the clear tube running from her bladder, emptying her urine into the clear bag they had tied to her bed rail.

"Ms. Simpson,, I'm Agent Bell of the FBI," the middle aged grey haired man said to her, showing her his badge. "Seems like we have a few things to discuss wouldn't you agree? Like how exactly we ended up here."

Mel looked over to the window and out at the sky. She was still a little woozy from the drugs but she nodded her head. She knew that no matter how many times she clicked her heels together and wished it wasn't happening, that they weren't going anywhere until they got some answers.

"First off let me say I'm glad you pulled through, you gave us a scare there. The last thing the BOP (Bureau of Prisons) want is to lose one on our watch. With that being said Ms. Simpson, my first question is, is there anything you want to tell me? Sometimes we can ask questions the wrong way, you know? Sometimes it's better and a little bit more comfortable when we just listen. So if you've got something to say, we're listening."

Mel looked at the aging man, unsure of what he expected her to say but she knew one thing he'd never hear from her lips; that Officer Connors was in any way connected to what happened to her.

"What is it you wanna know?" she said hoarsely, her throat scratchy from the ventilator.

"I wanna know how we reached this point," he said taking a seat beside her in the burgundy chair at the head of her bed. "How we ended up here with your life in jeopardy from the termination of a pregnancy, a pregnancy that under the current circumstances, shouldn't have happened. Can you explain that to me?"

Mel looked at the yellow tile on the wall to the left of her bed and felt a tear roll down the side of her face.

"It's simple. I fell for someone I shouldn't have. Not because he was a bad guy but because he was a bad guy," she chuckled softly to herself, coughing from the tickle in her throat. "He made me feel things I'd never felt before; made me feel so special. I thought that in my own crazy mind that we could be together once I got out so I jumped off the bridge for him," she said wiping her eyes. "I went head first for the idea of going off the compound with him," she lied. "It was my ex-boyfriend Mike. He would come pick me up from Leestown road after I would maneuver my way across the grass."

Mel stayed away from mentioning the hill below the camp or the Rec center. She didn't want them pulling any tapes and finding the car that
Connors had rented on camera.

"He picked me up a few times, we went somewhere secluded and had sex in his truck," she said, twirling the promise ring on her finger.

She knew at that moment that she would never lay eyes on the man she fell in love with again and Mel tried her best not to cry but she began to sob uncontrollably. She knew her journey was now heading to the FCI, taking her further from her family, Ella and possibly facing more time and charges. The exact same thing that could have happened had she chose to keep her child; so the pain she felt was a bit overwhelming for her. In her eyes, she'd lost all the way across the board.

Yet despite all, she did realize that she too had to take responsible for the part she played, decisions she'd made and the lives she altered. She looked at the burly agent who was taping her statement.

"This morning, he came back and met me on the road."

"And how exactly did you find out you were pregnant Ms. Simpson?"

"Well, I missed my period and so I needed a test."

"And did you go off the compound to get this test?"

"Yes, it's been a few weeks though... he bought one of those home stick tests and I just pee'd on the stick to find out," she said, knowing he was digging for information on inmates possible getting packages in on the compound.

"He came today and took me to an abortion clinic."

The agent asked which one and Mel knowing that they wouldn't find her name on record at any clinic, said she couldn't remember. If they wanted to prove anything against her other than what she was already admitting too, she'd let them do their own work. She had said all she was going to say.

The officer entered Ella's room with three clear plastic bags full of clothing, pictures, crafts and letters. The man stood in her doorway and asked her if he could come inside for a moment. Ella granted him entrance and he stood next to her locker out of view from the hallway.

As tears rolled down his face, he told Ella he was sorry.

"I never meant to hurt her. When I got to work and they told me that something had happened to her, I had to pretend like it didn't affect me but it did. It was the hardest acting job I'd ever had to pull off. I went in the restroom and I prayed so hard for her to be okay. My heart hurts so much for her right now and it hurts because I can't go to her and be with her. She has to face this alone and that's tearing me apart. I need to tell her I'm sorry and that I wish I would've never gone through with this, any of this."

Ella rolled her wheelchair over to Connors and grabbed him by the hand.

"They caught it in time so physically she's gonna be okay. Spiritually and mentally, it's gonna be a challenge for her to bounce back but Mel is strong. All we can do is pray, seek God's healing, ask for forgiveness and accept responsibility; all parties and then and only then can He step in and heal," she told him, handing him a Kleenex from the box on her locker.

"I know you don't believe me when I say this but... I love Melody, I truly do."

Ella looked at the picture of her and Mel that she had on her cork board.

"So do I, as if I birth that child myself. And I do know you care for her deeply but if you love her, truly love her like you say you do, then you've got to make decisions that are not only what's best for you but for her. Because I know she feels very strongly about you."

"And I for her and I also know its gonna get worse before it gets better," he said somberly, looking at her bags in the doorway. "She saved me, my job and my family. And in some ways I wish she hadn't. I'm gonna go and tell them everything tomorrow. I'm not going to allow her to pay for this all by herself."

"Listen to me, now I don't know you but I do know this; losing yo' job and family ain't gone change what happened nor will it stop what's happening now. This is what she wanted to do, to give you another chance at life with yo' family. Now what you choose to do with it is ultimately up to you but it's not what she wants for you.

The fact that you are here and packing out her things tells you that."

Connors took a deep breath and softly thanked Ella for the conversation. He tried his best to gather himself as he grabbed the clear trash bags and headed down to the office. He closed the door and sat down on the ledge of his desk. He had to go through her property piece by piece and separate the things that she could have shipped to her next facility, from the things that would have to be mailed home to her family.

He sat back in his chair, thoughts of her running rampant in his head. The radio did little to soothe his mood as he hesitantly began task at hand. He picked up the white cotton robe from the plastic, held it up to his face and inhaled her scent as the tears fell from his eyes. He could have lost her today for good; the thought hurt him so badly.

"...said I left my baby girl a message, said I won't be coming home, I'd rather be alone. She doesn't fully understand cause I'd rather leave than to cheat...."

What started as a simple game of sexual cat and mouse had disrupted so many lives. Ella was losing someone so close to her, he was losing someone he knew he shouldn't love but had come to love very deeply... and Mel, she was losing it all.

".. if she give me some time I can be the man she needs but there's a lot of lust inside of me and we've been together since our teenage years. I really don't mean to hurt her but I need some time to be alone..."

He picked up Mel's clothing and began to fold each piece, one by one, neatly on his desk. Normally when an inmate is packed out, all their things are just thrown into the bag with no regards to neatness but Connors took care to treat everything she owned special. He looked at her pictures, one by one before placing them neatly inside an envelope. He ran his finger over her face.

"...but when you love someone you just don't treat them bad. Oh how I feel so sad, now that I want to leave. She's crying her heart to me, how could you let this be? I just need time to see where I wanna be, where I wanna be..."

He kissed the photos and continued to pack away her things, taking the time to stick a note inside the pocket of a pair of her sweat pants.

Words can't express how I feel right now. Please know that it hurts me so much to know you're hurting like this. I love you and I never realized just how much I do until this moment.

"... never could I imagine, that you would play a major part in a decision that's so hard. Do I leave? Should I stay, should I go? I think about my life and what matters to me the most. Girl the love that we share is real but in time your heart will heal..."

As he tied knots in her bags to secure her belongings, Connors vowed to himself that he would continue to be there for her, continue to send money both to her and her mother, even look out for Ella when he could because he knew how important she was to Mel.

His cards however went unanswered for the first two months of Mel's stay at the FMC in Carswell, TX., until finally Mel was mentally strong enough to sit down and pen a letter to him. In this letter she released him from all responsibility... all the hurt, all the un-forgiveness and any loyalty he felt he owed to her.

Thank you so much for all you have done for me and my family. I truly, truly appreciate it but now it's time to let me go... to let us go... I want you to go and be the husband you sat out to be when you married the "true love" of your life. I'm still so in awe

240

that a man as wonderful as you, chose to love me but I also understand that as long as I continue to hold on to you, I'm keeping myself from being the woman God wants me to be.

He's been my rock in this dark place and He has blessed me to not receive any extra time for my actions. I get to go home soon, on time!

I will <u>ALWAYS</u> love you for who you have been to me, how you have been towards me and what I've learned being with you. Most importantly what I learned about myself. I know now that I deserve a man after God's own heart for me. Your touch has taught me that I deserve that touch, filled with all the passion, all the want and desire yours possessed. Kisses that make me feel that his lips were designed specifically for me! From the bottom of my heart I "thank you" for being the vessel He used to show me that I deserve it but from the man He has specifically chosen for me.

And that can't be you because He designed you for someone else. Now it's time for you to shower all that love onto the one who truly deserves it from you... your wife. Be the man we both know you are and the man God has ordained you to be. I only ask one thing of you... well two... never forget me and when you do think of me, have no regrets and smile for me.

Love you always and know that you will always, always have a special place in my heart. Now...go...be.. great! As I plan to do the same!

Luv Melody

Connors smiled as he read the contents of her letter. His heart hated to let her go but he too understood that he had too, if not for himself or his wife, than for her.

That was the true love Ella spoke of... loving her enough to know that he wasn't what was best for her and moving out of the way so God could bring along the man who was.

He kissed the letter as he pulled away from the post office parking lot and placed it in his shirt pocket. He silently said a prayer and asked God to watch over her as he turned onto Nandino Blvd., headed to his destination... to his wife and his brand new baby girl.... his family.

245

248

51738001R00137

Made in the USA
Charleston, SC
01 February 2016